S0-AGK-287

"Oh, my God," he cried. "I love you. I loved you from the first moment you came walking into that room . . . Don't be cruel to me!"

"Hush," Lydia said trembling. "You mustn't."

They stood looking at each other and, as their eyes met, some fierce passion held them spellbound. He drew her nearer to him and seized her in his arms. She felt his kisses—fierce, possessive, demanding. They swept her into the sky and the world was forgotten . . .

Also in Pyramid Books

by

BARBARA CARTLAND

The Bitter Winds of Love

by
Barbara Cartland

PYRAMID BOOKS 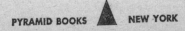 NEW YORK

THE BITTER WINDS OF LOVE
A PYRAMID BOOK

Copyright © 1976 by Barbara Cartland

All rights reserved. No part of this publication may be repro-
duced or transmitted in any form or by any means, electronic
or mechanical, including photocopy, recording, or any infor-
mation storage and retrieval system, without permission in
writing from the publisher.

Pyramid edition published May 1976

ISBN 0-515-03991-8

Printed in the United States of America

Pyramid Books are published by Pyramid Publications (Harcourt
Brace Jovanovich). Its trademarks, consisting of the word
"Pyramid" and the portrayal of a pyramid, are registered in
the United States Patent Office.

Pyramid Publications
(Harcourt Brace Jovanovich)
757 Third Avenue, New York, N.Y. 10017

"And fear which lurks in every heart
Blows like a bitter wind, when we
would find love."

CHAPTER ONE

1938

Lydia Bryant replaced the telephone receiver and stood still.

It was late in the afternoon and it was growing dark in the narrow well-like hall. The only light came from the roof, and the darkening sky shed a sombre unearthly dreariness through the rain-stained glass.

To Lydia it seemed as if she were entombed in this silent gloomy house which she had always hated. Then slowly to her mind came the thought that she was free.

She could not realize it; could not accept without question the news she had heard but a moment ago in the crisp military tones of her brother-in-law's voice.

"Donald died this morning," he said. "I am arranging for the funeral to take place on Friday. I will let you know further particulars later."

Donald was dead!

If she was honest with herself, she had been waiting for this; yet now that the moment was upon her, she could remember her husband only as she had first seen him—nearly seven years ago—tall, distinguished, looking down at her from his great height.

'How handsome he is!' she had thought as they had been introduced, and in those first seconds of their acquaintance when he had held her hand a little longer than was necessary.

It had been a swift courtship. Barely two months later Lydia had walked down the aisle of the little grey-stone country church, the wife of Donald Bryant. Thinking of him now, those first weeks of married life passed before her in a succession of happy memories.

Donald swimming beside her in the blue water of the

Mediterranean; sun-bathing on the hot rocks; laughing at her efforts at aquaplaning, and holding her closely in his arms—an ardent, possessive, always masterful lover.

She had loved him, yet in her affection there had always been a touch of fear, not only because of the disparity in their ages—as her friends had pointed out seventeen years was a big difference—but because there was something else which made her shrink from her husband, even in their most intimate and passionate moments.

Any young girl might have found Donald too ardent, almost unbalanced, in his lovemaking.

When the first rapturous days of their honeymoon were over, Lydia knew that while she reciprocated his adoration, her husband was still in many ways a stranger whom she feared rather than understood.

There was always something queer about him, she remembered now, but his headaches had come on gradually.

Then, preluded by moods of querulousness, of depression and unreasonable demands upon his wife, they grew worse, until, finally, he had become unrecognizable—a man who was hardly human, a monster from which she shrank terrified and trembling. . . .

Slowly, as though she were awakening from a nightmare which gripped her still, Lydia moved across the hall and opened the door which led into the Drawing-Room.

The curtains were not yet drawn to shut out the dismal wet landscape, but there was a fire burning brightly on the hearth, and it threw a glow of warm light into the room.

Once again she could hear the Doctor's gentle voice as he told her the London specialist's verdict after a prolonged examination.

"Your husband was only slightly wounded in the War, Mrs. Bryant," he said. "At the time it seemed so unimportant an injury that it was treated only at the Base hospital and he was not even invalided home. But that glancing piece of shrapnel dislodged a small bone and this is causing all the trouble today."

Seeing the hope die from Lydia's white face he added: "I am sorry but there is nothing we can do."

Even he did not realize that he was condemning a girl of twenty-one to a life of torture and torment. It was not only when Donald was in one of his moods that Lydia experienced agony.

There was the misery of anticipation, the wondering each time they were separated how he would be when they met again.

Sometimes, for three or four weeks he would be himself, normal, charming, considerate, and then would come the first signs that she grew to dread; the twitching of the fingers, the restlessness, arguments with the servants and a suspicious attitude towards their neighbors and anyone with whom she came into contact.

Every moment of her day would be spent in tense terror —often she would creep away to her room praying fiercely to herself.

"Let this pass, oh, God, let it pass—just this once. Do not let him get worse."

Yet always the storm would come, the raised voice, the violence and finally the aftermath of tears and repentance. As the years passed, Lydia grew to hate most of all the scenes of repentance.

There was something degrading about Donald groveling in misery. She grew even to prefer her bruises to the times when he tried to kiss them well again.

She felt herself growing colder, increasingly apart from her husband until finally, try as she would to evade the truth, she knew she hated him.

She wondered how long she could have continued to live with him, how long before her pride broke down and she appealed for help. But that humiliation was spared her.

Donald, in one of his wild rages when he was quite irresponsible for his actions, grievously injured one of the farm hands. He was taken away to a private nursing-home.

At first Lydia used to visit him there—his family expected this of her, and once a month she would set out, driving herself in the small car to where, high on a hill overlooking the valley where he had lived, Donald was virtually imprisoned.

Always as she drew nearer to the big, ugly, red-brick mansion Lydia found herself driving slower and slower.

She dreaded the interviews, disliking the days when Donald was most normal, more than when he hardly recognized her and seemed in no way related to the man she had loved and married.

Then gradually her visits began to upset him.

"I am afraid he is always worse when you come," the nurses told her.

Finally she was asked to stay away.

She had no-one to whom she could confide her relief that she was not wanted. Donald's immediate relatives were an elder brother and his wife.

They had never approved of the marriage, and while doing what they considered their duty towards their sister-in-law were not inclined to be intimate or friendly with her.

Donald's brother, Colonel Bryant, seldom sent Lydia a quarterly check without stressing how necessary and important was strict economy.

When finally he took over the management both of the house and of the estate, she was thankful, content to try and pay her own necessities with the small income she had of her own, which had been left her on the death of her parents.

An orphan since she was sixteen, Lydia had been brought up by her mother's brother, the Rector of a small Church in Shropshire.

He had died shortly after her second year of marriage, and with his passing she had found herself without relations except for a few distant cousins who were far too engrossed in their own lives to be interested in hers.

Only to Evelyn Marshall who had been her mother's friend did Lydia write and receive in return letters which in their deep affection and common sense brought her a breath of another world.

Mrs. Marshall also sent her books, and these became to Lydia the true companions and friends of her years of isolation.

It was an unreal life she lived—eating, sleeping and reading, surrounded only by the figures of her imagination, moving alone in the fastness of the silent house to which she had come eagerly and happily as a bride.

Who could have forseen at that moment that Donald would have become as she had last seen him—a beast

10

rather than a man, screaming and crying out against her, striving to injure her with mad, savage hands? . . .

A coal falling noisily into the grate startled her. She got to her feet, and, smoothing back her hair, turned on the light.

When she had done so she looked for a moment into the mirror which hung over the mantelpiece, staring at her own reflection, seeing two deep-blue eyes below dark hair drawn back from a broad forehead.

'I am twenty-seven,' Lydia thought to herself. 'Twenty-seven! And now I have to begin life again!'

The opening of the door startled her. She turned abruptly as if ashamed of being caught looking at herself. It was the manservant entering with the tea.

For a moment Lydia watched him arranging the silver teapot and putting down the plates of sandwiches and cakes that she rarely touched, then she said:

"I have had a message from Colonel Bryant, Marsham."

Quite suddenly and unexpectedly she could say no more. Her voice seemed arrested in her throat. Marsham, however, appeared to understand.

He looked at her and asked:

"It's the master, isn't it, Madam?"

Lydia nodded.

"The last time he was over the Colonel told me he was bad. I was expecting it, Madam."

He drew a deep breath, and Lydia knew that he was in the most correct and traditional fashion about to offer his condolences. Suddenly she felt she could not bear it.

With a cry she turned and ran from the room. She hurried up the staircase, feeling rather than seeing her way, and rushing blindly into her own bedroom she pushed the door behind her. It slammed.

Flinging herself on the bed Lydia found tears coursing down her cheeks, and she felt herself shaking all over with the fierce force of agonized weeping, but even while she cried, while she felt her control sweep from her, she knew that she wept in relief rather than bitterness.

"I am free," she sobbed. "I am free,"—and was shamed by the sound of her own voice.

CHAPTER TWO

Lydia, travelling towards Worcester, stared out of the railway carriage.

For the present she did not know what the future held. She only knew that as she came nearer to the home of Evelyn Marshall she felt hope and vitality stirring anew within her.

A dead weight seemed to have been lifted from her shoulders, the clouds of oppression were passing away and she felt young and for the first time for many years —eager.

Evelyn's response to the letter which bore the news that Lydia was at last free had been a telegram, abrupt and to the point:

> *"Expect you as soon as possible. Wire*
> *day of arrival, love, Evelyn."*

It was characteristic, Lydia thought with a little smile as she read it.

Evelyn always made up her mind quickly but with a thoroughness which brooked neither refusal nor argument.

Lydia, like most other people of Evelyn Marshall's acquaintance, was prepared unashamedly to lay the burden of her troubles on those capable shoulders and let her decide problems which at the moment to her seemed insurmountable.

When she married, Donald had told her frankly that it was imperative that they should have a child. All his money and property were entailed so that in the event of his not producing an heir everything reverted to his brother's family.

After seven years of married life, Lydia found herself with exactly what she had owned the day of her marriage. Two hundred pounds a year had been left by her father, but with fluctuations, her income was often considerably less.

She realized that she must shortly come to some decision as to her future. What was she to do? She felt singularly unfitted for any sort of work, but work she must.

Fifty years ago her only hope would have been a post as an underpaid governess, but nowadays a higher standard of schoolroom knowledge was required than any she could pretend to.

Her problem seemed a hopeless one, and Lydia was thankful that she could for the moment leave it in abeyance until she had seen Evelyn.

With any other friend whom one had not seen for so many years, preliminary conversation might have been difficult. But not so with Mrs. Marshall.

Before they had left the narrow streets of Worcester behind and were speeding out into the countryside, Lydia had already begun to tell her story to attentive and sympathetic ears.

They drove until they approached the high range of hills which towers above the scattered town of Malvern, then turned towards the flat valley where the wide Severn meets the narrow slow-moving Avon. There in a small hamlet of black and white cottages was Evelyn's home—'Four Arrows.'

Evelyn drove up to the oak porch, and as the car came to a standstill the door was opened by a smiling maid waiting to usher them in and take Lydia's luggage.

Evelyn switched off the engine and turned towards her guest:

"Welcome back to 'Four Arrows', darling," she said affectionately.

* * * *

Lydia woke to find the early autumn sunshine was struggling to force its way through the chintz curtains which veiled the casement windows of her room.

For some moments she lay, letting the events of yesterday steal into her mind. She felt happy and at peace with all the world.

Then with a sudden burst of energy she sprang from her bed and, walking barefooted over the blue-carpeted floor, pulled back the curtains.

Over the river the pale morning mists were disappearing, and far away in the distance the hills were silhouetted against a cloudless sky.

Lydia stood for a long time at the window until, with a sigh of contentment, she went away to seek her bath and breakfast. She felt that today held a promise for her of many things.

"Have you slept well?" Evelyn asked her, when she came downstairs.

Then added, as she saw a smile on the girl's face:

"You needn't answer that question, you look different this morning."

"I feel it," Lydia confessed. "Oh, Evelyn, darling, I am so glad to be here."

"And I am glad to have you," Evelyn replied.

When they had finished breakfast, they set off almost immediately in Evelyn's car to deliver some parcels at a hospital. Their errand done, Evelyn turned the car not homewards, but towards the hills.

"Are you taking me anywhere special?" Lydia asked, "or is this just a joy ride?"

"Somewhere special," Evelyn replied.

But she did not add any more, and Lydia was content not to press her for a further explanation, feeling that she would speak in her own good time.

They drove swiftly but carefully through narrow lanes and past small villages of charming old black-and-white houses until an ancient signpost told them that they were travelling in the direction of Little Goodleigh.

There was a small grey-stone Church set beside a village green, and there was a blacksmith's shop and a public-house which had evidently known the old days of coaches.

There were cottages with small, well-kept gardens, and beyond them iron gates which led into a short avenue of beech trees. One of the gates was open, and Evelyn drove her car up the drive until they came to the house.

With the morning sun glittering on the diamond panes

of its many windows, it was one of the most lovely houses Lydia had even seen in her life.

It was of the sixteenth century, without any sign of later buildings or reconstruction to spoil or deface it.

"What a wonderful house!" Lydia said. "Who lives here?"

As she spoke she realized that the house was uninhabited. Inside, the windows' oak shutters were drawn and barred. The front door was closed and padlocked on the outside, as though in double precaution against trespassers.

The garden which surrounded the house was in a state of neglect. There were weeds in the paths, and bushes and shrubs had thrust long, untidy arms in every direction.

"It is sad to see it empty, isn't it?" Evelyn said.

"One can't imagine anyone not wanting to live here," Lydia answered, "it's the most perfect place I have ever seen. Can't we go inside?"

Evelyn shook her head.

"I am afraid not," she replied.

"Tell me about it," Lydia commanded.

Evelyn drew up her car in the wide sweep before the front door and switched off the engine.

"This," she started, "is the Manor of Little Goodleigh, and the house, like most of the property around it, has been in the hands of the Carlton family since the house was built. General Carlton died five years ago, and since then the Manor has been shut up as you see it now, and not lived in.

"Isn't there an heir?" Lydia asked.

"There is," Evelyn replied; "the General had one son called Gerald, and he was brought up here, and I believe —in fact I am sure—that he loved this house as deeply as his father did."

"Then what happened to him?" Lydia asked. "Where is he now?"

"He is living abroad," Evelyn replied; "it's a long story, but I am going to tell you about it because indirectly it concerns yourself."

"Concerns me?" Lydia ejaculated, and then added: "No, I won't ask questions—tell me everything."

"When Gerald Carlton came of age," Evelyn said, "about

16

twelve years ago, there was a great party held here at the Manor. I came to it, and amongst all the festivities, the speech-making, the good wishes of the tenants and toast-drinking, the thing that struck me most was the genuine devotion of Gerald to his father and mother.

"It was not surprising, for Mrs. Carlton was one of the most beloved and charming women it was possible to meet, and her husband was popular wherever he went.

"It was obvious that there was an unusually deep tie between them and their son, who had been born when neither of them were very young. The General spent most of his life abroad, and they had waited for many years before starting a family.

"I left the party that evening thinking that here in this house there was a united family love it did one good to see, and yet, only a year later, this was to be shattered, broken up by a woman.

"About five miles away from here is Taverel Castle, owned by Sir John Taverel who, in those days, was Master of the Hounds, and one of the most important people in the county.

"It must have been out hunting that young Gerald met Lady Taverel, for his parents did not bother to see much of their more dashing and sophisticated neighbors.

Margaret Taverel was lovely. "She was younger than her husband by a great many years, but must, I suppose, have been about thirty-five.

"She had golden hair and deep-blue eyes which had turned the heads of many young men at one time or another, and at first people were inclined to laugh when Gerald Carlton showed his devotion very obviously, and followed her around wherever she went.

"Sir John was a busy man, and a somewhat difficult one to understand or to get to know. I can't say that he minded his wife having admirers. He took little notice of them, and if he remonstrated with her in private, he made no public demonstration.

"Gerald, being young was, perhaps, more ostentatious in his devotion than the other men, more experienced, had been. Anyway, in a very short while, the whole neighborhood was gossiping, although few people, I think, thought it was a serious matter.

"I had known Margaret for many years. I liked her, although, quite frankly, I thought her one of the stupidest women I have ever met. But I could not deny her beauty and graciousness, which made her attractive and charming to everyone whom she met.

"She came to see me one day, and while we were still talking Gerald was announced. She obviously expected him, whilst his visit was a complete surprise to me, and just for a moment their delight at meeting each other and the irrepressible joy on both their faces, gave me a moment's anxiety.

"I thought my fears were ridiculous. Gerald was a mere child, and Margaret a woman approaching middle age. I watched them drive away together, and returning to the house dismissed the whole episode from my mind.

"Two days later I heard the news that they had run away together. To say I was astonished was to put it mildly. It was the last thing I, at any rate, had ever dreamt of, although I had known Gerald since he was a child, and Margaret Taverel for nearly as many years.

"General and Mrs. Carlton were heartbroken, but they, like everybody else, waited to see what action Sir John would take in the matter. What shocked people most was the fact that there was a child nearly seven years old, a girl, and I had always believed that Margaret was devoted to little Ann.

"In telling you this story, Lydia, I can't help making it sound as though I blamed Margaret for what occurred. In some ways it is impossible not to; she was an older woman, while Gerald had hardly qualified to be called a man; it is only fair to say that now I can see her point of view.

"She was still lovely; still longing for love and romance as ardently as she had fifteen years earlier when she had married Sir John. I am quite prepared to believe that their marriage was a failure before she met Gerald.

"He was a difficult man to live with. He had distinct intellectual qualities. Margaret was a fool, but a very lovely one—that was all she had to offer any man, a beautiful face and an exquisite body.

"She asked very little from life, really, just flattery and admiration, and a man to make a fuss of her, and none of these things could she obtain from her husband.

18

"Margaret was afraid of growing old in the pomposity and grandeur of Taverel Castle. Gerald's youth and good looks swept her off her feet, and she ran away with him without thinking, without reasoning or considering what might come of her action."

Evelyn paused, and opening her handbag, took out a cigarette.

"What did happen?" Lydia asked.

"Nothing, just nothing," Evelyn replied; "that was the tragedy."

"But didn't Sir John divorce her?"

"No, he refused, even though finally General Carlton himself went to see him and begged him to do so."

"How awful," Lydia said. "What did they do?"

"They lived abroad," Evelyn answered, "and at first I think they were very happy. Then, after two years, the tragedy happened. They were in Cairo, and Margaret was out riding when her horse slipped and rolled on her."

"Was she killed?" Lydia asked.

"It would, perhaps, have been better if she had been. No, she was not killed, but her spine was badly injured, and Gerald was told that Margaret could never walk again.

"It must have been an awful moment for him, not only for himself, but faced with the task of telling a woman who cared not only for her looks and her loveliness that for the rest of her life she would be an invalid.

"They bought a house just outside Cairo, and there they have lived ever since. Three years ago Sir John died; immediately afterwards they were married."

Evelyn paused and looked out of the window at the Manor.

"By that time," she said, "both Gerald's parents were dead also, and I always feel myself that they would have been happier if they could have known that their son was legally married. They knew, too, that as long as the union was unblessed Gerald would never return home."

"Has he come back since?" Lydia asked.

"No," Evelyn answered. "I think perhaps it would make him too sad to see this house, unless of course, he has altered very much in the passing years, and no longer cares."

"But how does this affect me?" Lydia questioned, unable to restrain her curiosity any longer.

"You will remember," Evelyn said slowly, "that I spoke about the child that Margaret left behind, Ann Taverel. She was seven then, now she is just eighteen. She was, of course, brought up by her father, who left, in his will, trustees and guardians for her until she should reach the age of eighteen.

"After that he had no power to prevent her going to her mother should she wish to do so.

"At the end of this month Ann sails for Cairo to meet the mother that she has not seen for eleven years. She has made up her mind that she will, for the present, make her home with Margaret.

"Last week, just two days before I heard from you, I had a letter from Margaret asking me to find someone to look after Ann, not only to take her out there, but to remain as chaperone and companion to the girl.

"I was wondering who would be suitable for the post when your letter arrived, and I knew that there was a direct answer to my problem. That is why I have brought you here today and told you this story. I wanted you to know the whole truth before you met Ann."

"But Evelyn," Lydia expostulated, "can I look after a young girl? Am I capable or suitable?"

Evelyn smiled affectionately and put her hand on Lydia's arm.

"I consider you both," she said, "and while I hope you will be a good influence on Ann, I think that she, as well as Cairo's society, would be a good education for you."

Lydia laughed. It was so like Evelyn.

"A mutual benefit society," she said, and then added seriously: "it sounds rather frightening."

"Nobody could be frightened of Margaret Carlton," Evelyn said firmly. "Of Gerald I can't tell you anything. When I last saw him he was a very charming, cheerful boy of twenty-two. He is now a man of nearly thirty-four."

"Tell me about Ann," Lydia asked.

"She's a darling," Evelyn answered enthusiastically. "Very pretty, very impulsive, and used to getting her own way."

"Oh, dear!" Lydia sighed.

20

"But you shall judge for yourself," Evelyn said, throwing away her cigarette and starting up the engine of the car. "Ann is coming to tea to-day, and you can make all your plans with her."

"But suppose she doesn't like me," Lydia said nervously.

"She will," Evelyn answered confidently.

Turning the car, they drove down the drive leaving the Manor alone to its shuttered silence.

CHAPTER THREE

Ann was lovely, there was no doubt about it.

She pirouetted slowly before Lydia and Evelyn, showing off a new green tulle evening dress which billowed out from her slim waist and yet revealed, rather than concealed, the lissom, slender lines of her young figure.

She was dining out with a young man at Ciros, leaving Lydia and Evelyn alone at the hotel where they were all staying.

After three days which had been one long hectic rush, Lydia was looking forward to a quiet evening when she could go to bed early and rest—even if she did not sleep.

She had found it difficult to sleep the last few nights, for she had been so excited by the events which had followed rapidly one upon the other that at times she felt this could not be happening to her quiet, prosaic self, but to some stranger.

From the moment that Evelyn had introduced her to Ann at 'Four Arrows' she had not had a moment to herself. Ann had arrived at the house with the news that she intended to sail for Cairo in a week's time, with or without a chaperone.

Fortunately, she took an immediate liking to Lydia, and there was no need for Evelyn to oppose this decision, as she would undoubtedly have done had there been any real possibility of Ann sailing alone.

Although she was eighteen, fair fluffy hair and immense pale-blue eyes made Ann Taverel look younger, and only the sophistication of very crimson lipstick and scarlet fingernails made a casual onlooker take her for more than a schoolgirl.

One did not need to be many moments in Ann's company without realizing that she was attractive, with charming manners and the gift of making most people whom she met like her very much, and that apart from a natural impulsiveness she was not gifted with brains.

Like her mother, Ann's head was ruled entirely by her heart, and after a very short time Lydia found herself wondering what would happen when the girl's emotions were genuinely aroused.

At the moment she was excited, flattered, and not a little amused by the attention she was receiving from the score or more of young men who fluttered around her in the proverbial fashion of moths around a candle.

"She is only a child yet," Evelyn said more than once to Lydia.

But her tone was anxious, and Lydia knew that she was worried about the future of fascinating little Ann.

All day long the telephone would be ringing, servants would be kept busy bringing notes and flowers, or announcing young men, who arrived prepared to wait patiently for hours, if need be, until Ann could spare them her attention.

When Ann had made it quite clear that she intended to go to Cairo on Tuesday week, and that she had already cabled her mother to that effect, Evelyn accepted the inevitable with a smile, and offered to do all she could to facilitate their departure.

"You are a darling!" Ann said to her, putting her arms round her neck and giving her a hug. "I don't know what I should do without you, Aunt Evelyn; but then, doesn't everyone within a radius of fifty miles say that to you at least seven times a week?"

"It's easy to flatter me, now you have got your own way," Evelyn replied, smiling at the girl affectionately, so that her words held no sting in them.

"Is that all right for you, Lydia?" asked Ann. "Can you be ready on Tuesday?"

"Oh, quite easily," Lydia replied. "I have got nothing particular of my own to see to."

"Nothing to see to," echoed Evelyn Marshall, with a little cry. "My dear Lydia, you don't think you can go to Cairo without any clothes?"

"Why, no, perhaps I can't. I didn't think of it," Lydia confessed rather shamefacedly.

She had grown so used to wearing anything which came to hand, and was comfortable, that she had forgotten how necessary and what an important part clothes play in the life of the average woman.

"We go to London to-morrow," Evelyn said firmly.

As Lydia agreed, Evelyn took pencil and paper, and started to make a list of the things she would require.

After half an hour Lydia expostulated:

"But it's ridiculous, Evelyn, I can't take the job if I require so much. We haven't the time to get them, and what is more I certainly haven't the money to pay for them."

"That's my affair," Evelyn said with a smile. "They are going to be my present to you, a trousseau in which to start your new life."

"I wouldn't hear of it," Lydia answered. "It's very, very sweet of you, but of course I can't take such a present."

"And since when have you become so proud?" Evelyn questioned. "My dear, for nearly seven years I have been denied your company and the pleasure of giving you presents and parties. What I should have spent in actual money, if you like to put it that way, has accumulated, and now it is going to be spent all at once.

"You are going to Cairo because it is a marvellous opportunity which may never present itself again, and if you think I can send out to Margaret and Gerald a chaperone for Ann looking like a scarecrow, you're wrong. I have my own reputation to think of, you must remember, and you go as my friend."

She said these last words humorously, but Lydia could not laugh with her. She felt tears sting her eyes, and there was a lump in her throat at this unexpected kindness and generosity.

She tried to stammer her thanks, but Evelyn hushed the words away, and continued adding to the list of necessary purchases, which grew longer every minute.

After forty-eight hours in London Lydia came to the conclusion that while she would have plenty of clothes to take to Cairo, she personally would arrive a wreck.

The hours of standing to be fitted, the struggling in the

crowded shops before one could get attention, and the noise and bustle in the streets, exhausted her, even while the novelty of it all kept her excited and nervously alert.

Under the capable hands of a London hairdresser her hair was trimmed and re-dressed in a new and fashionable way, although it retained the simplicity which suited her so well.

"Aunt Evelyn, she will be the belle of Cairo!" Ann exclaimed, when she returned to the hotel.

"And that will be very good for your conceit," Evelyn answered.

There could hardly have been a more satisfactory contrast than that between Lydia and Ann. Ann's loveliness was that of a rosebud. She was fresh and exquisite in a dress of filmy tulle, of crisp colored muslin surmounted by a large-brimmed hat trimmed with flowers and ribbons.

Sheathlike dresses of heavy crepe and velvet which clung to Lydia's more sophisticated figure, gave her both poise and an illusive form of glamour difficult to describe, but very perceptible.

Every day the happiness and adventure of the new life was bringing a fresh beauty to her expression, and while her general appearance might make her in some ways seem older than her years, there was a young and eager light to be found in her eyes.

"I can't believe it's true," she said to Evelyn a hundred times a day.

CHAPTER FOUR

It was not until Ann and Lydia started on their journey that Lydia realized how much was to be required of her in this new job.

The final hustle of getting off from the hotel to the train, the seeing to their luggage, the tipping of porters and the arranging of carriages, were all left in Lydia's hands.

From the moment that she walked into Ann's bedroom and found her only half-dressed when they should have been starting for the station, she was aware that she had to deal with someone without any sense of organization, and incapable of looking after herself or her belongings.

Ann didn't fuss about anything.

She just looked beautiful and managed not only to be invariably late, so that Lydia was in a constant state of anxiety lest they should be left behind, but also to mislay her tickets, her notecase, and, finally, her handbag.

Had it not been for Evelyn, who remained capable and practical in any circumstances, however trying, they would not have departed for Cairo that day.

But somehow, panting and exhausted, Lydia managed to get herself and her charge into the train, and as the carriage door closed upon them, the train started.

"I am sure we have forgotten something," Ann said, pulling her soft felt hat from her curly fair head, and taking out a mirror to look at herself.

"It will certainly be your fault if we have," Lydia longed to reply.

But there was something so ingenuous about Ann that the sharp words she could have spoken died on her lips, and instead she laughed.

"I hope you realize," she said, "that your dressing-case is not packed, the things are just thrown into it. I expect every bottle is broken."

Ann shrugged her shoulders.

"I didn't get to bed until three o'clock last night," she said. "I am dead tired this morning, I just could not get up."

"I really ought to be very angry with you," Lydia said. "If we had missed this train we should have wasted our sleepers to Marseilles, and might even have missed the boat."

"Well, we haven't, anyway," Ann said, "so don't bother to lecture me, as I shan't listen."

She smiled as she spoke and Lydia knew that her task of chaperone and companion was going to be no easy one.

They had not progressed far on the journey before Lydia found Ann had definite ideas about whiling away the boredom of the railway journey. She scrutinized the travellers all the way to Dover, and when they arrived on the ship announced:

"I am going to have a look around to see who is aboard."

She left Lydia in the cabin, thankful to lie down and close her eyes, not because she was feeling seasick—it was a calm day—but because she was sleepy.

She had not slept the night before, and had been up since seven o'clock packing her own clothes and trying to ensure, without avail, against a last-minute rush.

Ann was away a long time, and Lydia awoke with a guilty start just before they docked at Calais to find she was still alone in the cabin.

She put on her hat and, glancing at herself in the little mirror hanging on the wall, was aware that the rest and sleep had taken away the lines of tiredness under her eyes, and made her look fresh and young.

Lydia went in search of Ann and found her hanging over the rail on the windward side of the ship, deep in conversation with a tall, good-looking man.

As Lydia hesitated before approaching them, Ann turned and saw her.

"Are you looking for me?" she called out.

"We shall be in, in a few minutes," Lydia replied.

There was a pause while she waited for Ann to effect an introduction. To her surprise, the girl moved towards her and, slipping her arm through hers said:

"Well, I'll come and help you get the things ready," then, turning to her companion, she said: "We'll see you on the train, shan't we?"

"You most certainly will," come the reply. "Until then, *au revoir*."

"How nice for you to find a friend," Lydia said, when they were out of earshot. "Who is he?"

"I haven't the slightest idea!" Ann replied.

"Ann!" Lydia ejaculated in shocked tones. "You don't mean to say that you have never met that man before!"

"But of course not," Ann said, "we just got into conversation, or rather, he spoke to me and I answered. After all, travelling is the one time one can legitimately 'pick up' strangers."

The girl was so calm and possessed that Lydia felt her rather shocked feelings were absurd.

"I am sure your mother would not like it," she managed to say at last, feebly.

"We shall have to ask her," Ann replied cheerfully, "but I don't suppose she will care. Everyone talks to anybody these days without waiting for introductions."

"I think it might be rather dangerous," Lydia said.

Ann laughed.

"Darling," she said, "you are too old-fashioned, you make a drama out of the most ordinary and commonplace things."

For the moment Lydia was silent. She could think of nothing else to say, although inwardly she accused herself of being a feeble and ineffective guardian.

When, however, they boarded the train and were joined in their coupe by the stranger, who asked very politely if he might have tea with them, she felt that she ought to have said more and not been so weak.

Ann, she told herself, was an heiress, besides having a certain social status, and in her position as chaperone she had no right to let the child make chance acquaintances of this sort. At the same time it would have been impossible to stop Ann, short of making a scene and being painfully insulting to the young man.

He seemed harmless enough. Dark and good-looking, he was going to Paris on business, although what that business was he did not specify.

Anyway, he and Ann chatted away together on all sorts of subjects, and he insisted on paying for all three teas when the meal was finished.

For an hour or so Lydia let her fears be lulled by the knowledge that, after Paris, they would be free of him, and there would be not much likelihood of meeting him again.

But shortly after this she heard he and Ann exchanging addresses, and promising to write to each other.

"You must tell me your first impressions of Cairo," the stranger said. "It is years since I went there, but I enjoyed every moment of it."

"Why don't you come out again?" Ann asked, with a provocative glance of her blue eyes.

"I shall give the suggestion my serious consideration," he promised.

It was not exactly what they said, but the exchange of glances which expressed far more than words.

'Oh, dear,' Lydia thought miserably, 'I ought to do something about this.'

She wished with all her heart that Evelyn was with them.

"Only another half an hour to Paris," she said brightly. "Is your seat far away, Mr. —?" she hesitated, then added: "I am afraid I didn't catch your name."

"My name is Henderson," he said, "Angus Henderson. Perhaps I had better be going back to my seat, but I have a splendid idea, if only you would agree."

"What is it?" Ann asked.

"You will have two or three hours in Paris before you have to catch your sleeper at the Gare de Lyons. Won't you come to the Ritz and have a cocktail with me?"

"I am afraid we have already made arrangements," Lydia said firmly, before Ann could speak. "Thank you very much, all the same."

"Nonsense," Ann interrupted, "of course we haven't, Lydia, and you know it! We would love to come," she said to Angus Henderson. "I think we shall have to take two

30

taxis, because we have got so much luggage, but we will meet you at the Ritz Bar as soon as we can."

"Then that's arranged," he said without looking at Lydia.

When he left the coupe there was a little silence between the two women. At last, Lydia broke it, choosing her words with care.

"I think you are making a mistake," she said. "We don't know anything about this young man, and we have no right to accept his hospitality."

"If we had met him at a private dance," Ann said, "and been introduced casually, you would not make the slightest fuss, and we should know just as little about him."

"Nevertheless," Lydia said, "I don't think it is right."

"Very well," Ann answered, "I shall go and have a drink with him, and you needn't."

"Don't be ridiculous," Lydia said sharply, "you know I couldn't let you go alone."

"Then we'll go together," Ann said firmly, "and enjoy ourselves, so don't be a spoil sport."

'I wonder what I ought to do,' Lydia thought to herself as they drove to the Ritz Bar.

She felt she could not cope with Ann in this mood, or indeed with the situation, which was one she had never anticipated. She felt that it was ridiculous for her to be opposed by a girl of eighteen.

When they arrived at the Ritz they found Angus Henderson waiting for them, accompanied by another man whom he introduced as Major Harold Taylor.

"I have just met Harry by chance," he said, "and where do you think he's off to? Cairo! He's travelling on your train to-night."

"How lovely," Ann said, and she shot a mischievous glance at Lydia to see how she liked the idea.

By this time Lydia had decided to let Ann have her head, and she smiled sweetly both at Angus Henderson and his friend, and accepted a champagne cocktail.

Major Taylor was older than Angus, and had that hard, wiry look of a man who has spent a great many years in the tropics.

He had a quiet voice and a dry sense of humor which made Lydia laugh two or three times, and she found herself liking him, and, indeed, being quite glad that there was a likelihood of their seeing a great deal more of him.

Ann and Angus Henderson were keeping up a flow of youthful badinage combined with a wordy flirtation that asked no help either from herself or Major Taylor, so that gradually they found themselves talking intimately together. Lydia confessed that this was her first trip abroad for many years.

"Are you going to stay long?" he asked.

"It depends very much on Miss Taverel," Lydia replied.

"Taverel!" Major Taylor said, "I didn't catch the name before. Is she any relation to Margaret Taverel, Gerald Carlton's wife?"

"Her daughter," Lydia answered.

"Good heavens!" he ejaculated, "Gerald's stepdaughter. Well, I would not have believed it. He will fiind . . ."

He stopped, as if afraid that the remark he was about to make would be indiscreet.

"You were going to say?" Lydia prompted, in curiosity.

"I was just surprised, that's all," the Major evaded.

He looked at Ann with a new interest.

"Do you know Mr. and Mrs. Carlton well?" Lydia asked.

"One cannot be long in Cairo without knowing Gerald," was the reply, and then Major Taylor added: "I can't imagine you two added to the household."

"Why not?" Lydia asked sharply.

She felt that while his words were innocent, he was in some way insinuating what would be best left unsaid.

"What are you talking about?" Ann interrupted suddenly.

"Major Taylor knows your mother and stepfather," Lydia replied.

"Oh, how exciting," Ann said. "Tell me about them. They are absolute strangers to me, of course, as I expect Lydia has told you."

"Strangers to you!" Major Taylor echoed in bewilderment. He looked from Ann to Lydia and back again. "Well, I shall leave it to be a surprise."

"The house or my parents?" Ann asked, "or both?"

Major Taylor laughed.

"I think I have chosen my words wrongly," he said.

"The person who is going to get the surprise in this case is Gerald. He has no idea, I am quite sure, that two such lovely creatures are *en route*."

Ann made a few more remarks, then turned her attention again to Angus Henderson, but Lydia stayed thoughtful.

'What does all this mean?' she asked herself. 'What was there strange about Gerald Carlton?'

CHAPTER FIVE

Harold Taylor had led a strange life which had accentuated the introspective urge in his character.

But as some women grow more beautiful as they grow older, so age to Harry Taylor brought a mellowness and a charm that he had never possessed in his youth.

It was probable that within the next five years he would command his Regiment, and in spite of the late development of his personality and his reserve, the younger officers and the men, because they believed in him, welcomed the idea.

Women had played a small part in his life. There had, of course, been many who would have liked to have aroused his interest. There had been bets in India as to whom would be the first to succeed, but all had failed.

His reserve enveloped him like an armour. People failed to realize that beneath his apparent coldness there was the shyness of a small boy.

As he became older, gradually his thoughts of women made him seek an ideal, a woman combining the virtues of the mother he had never known and the sensitive man's dream of wifely tenderness.

The night after he met Lydia he lay awake in the sleeper, and as the train jerked, banged and whistled its way towards Marseilles, he thought of her and of the house to which she was going, and he could not sleep.

Lydia, too, lay sleepless. The communicating door between her compartment and Ann's was open: the girl was fast asleep.

"I can always sleep in a train," Ann had assured her, as they undressed.

"You are lucky," Lydia replied.

"Perhaps it is an easy conscience," Ann had laughed back.

The words, recurring to Lydia as she lay awake, made her wonder about Ann's conscience.

'What did Ann really think about life, about herself, about this adventure in which she had involved Lydia, of meeting the mother she had not seen since she was a child?"

Again she thought of Major Taylor and his surprise at the thought of the two of them joining the Carlton household.

After a while she slept fitfully, waking every hour or so to find herself still being rattled through the darkness, the train moving terrifyingly fast, continually drawing up in jerks as they neared a station.

Finally, she fell into the deep sleep of exhaustion, and when she opened her eyes it was dawn.

In another hour they would be into Marseilles. Ann was already awake, had drawn up the blind, and was sitting on the end of her bed, looking out of the window, a warm dressing-gown draped round her shoulders.

She looked very young, with her fair hair in a halo of curls round her head, and Lydia, as she watched her, felt a kind of protective tenderness creep over her.

She hoped that Ann would never suffer as she had done; never have her youth swept from her in agony and terror, and realize, as the years passed by, that there was no way to freedom.

Ann turned her head and, seeing that Lydia was awake, smiled.

"Have you slept well?" she asked.

"Not a wink!" Lydia answered, "but then everybody says that in a train."

"It is bitterly cold," Ann said, "and there is no sign of the sun."

"We shall find sunshine in Cairo, though," Lydia replied reassuringly.

"Cairo!" Ann echoed. "Yes, I suppose we shall. Do you know, Lydia, I have always wanted to go to Egypt. I think I must have been an Egyptian in my last reincarnation."

Lydia laughed.

"You certainly don't look like one!" she said.

36

"All the same," Ann answered, "I feel an affinity with the country and with the people. I can't explain it, but when I get there I shall know that I have been there before."

"And if you feel that," Lydia said, still laughing, "I am quite certain you will believe you have been a Pharaoh or a Queen. I have never met anyone yet who remembered their previous incarnation as a char-woman or a peasant! They were always Kings and Queens, or Rulers of the earth!"

"I think you are horrid," Ann said, "and if I recognize myself in one of the tombs I shan't tell you."

"If you were one of the slaves who helped build the Pyramids," Lydia answered, "you certainly didn't have a tomb!"

But Ann refused to answer this last sally, and started to dress.

By the time they reached Marseilles the pale sun was flooding the town, but there was a bitter wind which made them glad that they had brought warm coats. Ann's was of fur, and with a big collar pulled up around her neck, only the tip of her nose and her bright eyes could be seen.

'How pretty she is!' Lydia thought for the thousandth time since they had started the journey, as she watched her charge walk down the station to bid Major Taylor 'good morning'.

She watched his courteous reply, and wondered if he would be Ann's next victim. Almost in spite of herself she hoped not. He is too nice, she thought, and too serious. He would never flirt and forget as Ann will.

None the less, she did not believe that Ann's smiles could be ignored.

It was with surprise when they finally got aboard the boat that she found Major Taylor constantly at her own side, bringing her books and papers, and tucking a warm rug firmly around her as she sat on deck watching the coast slowly recede into the distance.

He sat beside her in silence, and she found his presence peaceful, while she was curious as to the man himself and what he really thought.

Ann managed, before three days were passed, to scrape

37

acquaintance with a great number of people, both young and old.

There was no-one particularly interesting travelling, but Ann made the best of those there were, and Lydia was certain that at least one young tea-planter returning to Ceylon would have a broken heart.

The ship was late in arriving at Port Said.

By the time Ann and Lydia finally got off, had said good-bye to the friends they had made on board, and started in the train for Cairo, it was already early afternoon.

It was nearly six o'clock when they arrived at Cairo station, and here Ann and Lydia expected to be met by Gerald Carlton.

As the train steamed into the station Ann hung out of the window ready to guess, in her impetuous way, who among the people awaiting the passengers' arrival would be her stepfather.

"Do you think that's him?" she asked, pointing to a tall man with a small, fair moustache and a somewhat military bearing.

Major Taylor looked in the direction that she indicated.

"No, that is not your stepfather," he replied, "that's one of the A.D.C.s at the Embassy. A nice boy—you will doubtless meet him in a day or two. He is noted as the gayest young man in Cairo."

"Well, who's that then?" Ann asked, pointing to some-one else.

Again she was disappointed, and when finally they got out of the train she and Lydia realized that there was no one to meet them; apparently not even a car.

Major Taylor was obviously as surprised as they were, but he said nothing, merely offered to take them to the house in a taxi.

Lydia agreed; she felt depressed and a little despondent at this cold welcome.

It seemed strange when she and Ann had travelled so many thousands of miles to come here that Gerald Carlton could not even arrange to be at the station to greet them.

Nevertheless, she answered Ann's complaints calmly

and tried to make excuses which even in her own ears rang false.

It was exciting being in Cairo. Strange to see in the modern streets with its tramways and cars an occasional camel ambling along carrying a heavy load on its back and led by a small turbaned boy walking barefooted on the tarmac road.

Women veiled in yashmaks were chatting to each other, shuffling along the pavements in heelless leather shoes. Lydia and Ann leant forward in the taxi, staring out of the windows, exclaiming to each other at the distant minarets, the bullock-drawn carts, the gaily-coated dragomen.

"It is much too modern, really," Ann said in disappointed tones. "Why, we might be in the suburbs of London or any provincial town in England."

Major Taylor laughed.

"Wait until you see the Muski—the native bazaar," he said. "You will find it Oriental enough there!"

"I hope so," Ann started to say, when, with an exclamation, she cried: "Look! The Nile!"

They passed over the wide modern bridge which leads from the town into Gezira, and below them the great river shimmering in the sunlight flowed between verdant green banks.

"Here we are!" Major Taylor said as the taxi turned in at a wide gate and drove up a short drive bordered with bushes and flowering trees and stopped at the front door of a large white house.

There were a number of cars already parked in the drive, and after they had rung the bell, some moments elapsed before the door was opened by a white-garbed servant.

"Good-bye!" Major Taylor said, holding out his hand.

"But you must come in," Ann expostulated.

"I won't, if you don't mind," he replied. "I have got a lot of people to see even before I begin my unpacking, so will you make my apologies to your mother and say I will call another day."

"Good-bye," Lydia said, holding out her hand.

Major Taylor took it and held it tightly. He did not speak, but there was a look in his eyes which made Lydia

39

drop hers, and she turned swiftly and went from him into the house.

They followed the servant down dimly-lit passages until he opened a door and let them precede him into the room.

There were bursts of laughter and the chatter of voices, and for a moment Ann and Lydia stood bewildered on the threshold of a large room which seemed filled with people.

There were huge windows along one side of the room opening on to a verandah. At the far end, was a large bar around which a group of men and women were waiting for the drinks being deftly shaken for them by a white-coated barman.

Two or three people near the door broke off their conversation as Ann and Lydia entered, but they did not come forward to greet them, only stared with curious appraising eyes at the new-comers.

It seemed to Lydia that they stood there for ages, waiting and looking around them. Then she heard an exclamation from a tall man at the other end of the room. He came hurrying across to them.

"Good God!" he said, "it's Wednesday and I have been getting the days muddled again."

He came towards Ann, holding out both his hands.

"It is Ann, isn't it?" he said. "I was expecting you to-morrow. I must be mad. Can you ever forgive me for not meeting you at the station?"

"Yes, it is Ann," she answered rapidly recovering her composure now that she had attracted attention, "and we are perfectly furious with you!"

"Oh, don't say that," her stepfather answered.

He held out his hand to Lydia.

"Mrs. Bryant," he said, "I hope you, too, are not angry with me!"

Lydia looked at him. He was tall, fair, and heavily built, with square shoulders above a strong athletic body.

He was sunburnt, clean-shaven, handsome, and the blue eyes looking at her had in them an expression of charm.

"We were only disappointed," she answered.

"Where's my mother?" Ann asked.

"She is upstairs," Gerald Carlton replied. "She never comes to my—our parties. They make her head ache. Will you go up to her, or shall I take you?"

40

"I will find my own way," Ann answered swiftly.

Lydia realized that Ann wanted this reunion, after eleven years, to take place without the presence of strangers.

"Come and have a drink then, Mrs. Bryant," Gerald said, steering her through the crowd towards the bar.

"I won't, thank you," Lydia answered, but he laughed at her refusal.

"You are in the East now," he said; "you have to learn to drink at sundown—if at no other time."

"And who can teach you better than Gerald?" said a voice, and a woman detached herself from the throng and came towards them.

She was very small and exceedingly blonde, with sharp features and a shrill, ultra-sophisticated voice.

"This is Nina," Gerald said to Lydia.

"What a way to introduce me! Really, Gerald, you might make a good impression at first, at any rate."

"Oh, Mrs. Bryant will soon gain her own impressions," Gerald answered.

Nina put her head up towards him and said in a small, intimate voice:

"It's as you wish!"

Lydia felt embarrassed. It was obvious that Nina was flirting with Gerald Carlton and regarded her opinion as of little consequence. She made a movement towards the door and said in a clear and determined voice:

"Do you mind if I go up to my room? I would rather like to wash and change after the train journey."

Gerald began to argue, but Nina interrupted him.

"Don't be silly, darling," she said, "the poor girl wants to powder her nose! And why shouldn't she, I would like to know? Tessa!"

She called the name loudly. From another corner of the room a small child of about eight answered her.

"Coming, Mummy!"

She was a pretty child with fair hair framing a piquant face.

"Take Mrs. Bryant to her room," her mother commanded as she approached. "I can't remember which one she is to have, but Mohammed will know."

"All right," said Tessa.

41

Turning towards Lydia, she added with a ludicrously grown-up air:

"Will you follow me?"

Lydia smiled at the assurance of the child, but she wondered what authority her mother had in the house and why it was her business to allot the bedrooms.

Outside the door, away from the noise, the chatter and the smell of cigarette smoke, Lydia gave a sigh of relief.

"Are you tired?" Tessa asked, looking at her with inquisitive eyes.

"I am a bit," Lydia answered with a smile. "There are such a lot of people here, aren't there?"

Tessa shrugged her thin shoulder.

"There's always a lot of people here," she said. "Mummy likes crowds and so does Gerald."

"Do you and your Mummy live here?" Lydia asked, feeling that she ought not to question the child, at the same time bewildered by the household.

"For the moment," Tessa answered, "and I suppose we shall stay until Mummy gets bored. It's not bad," she added as an afterthought.

"I am sure it isn't," Lydia answered, somewhat taken aback at this frank criticism.

By this time they had climbed the wide polished stairs to a landing where Tessa opened one of the doors and showed Lydia a small room opening on to a verandah with an exquisite view over the garden, which sloped away towards the banks of the Nile.

"This is your room," she said. "I expect Mohammed will bring up the luggage when he has got time."

"I hope so," Lydia answered. "I would like to have my dressing-case."

"All right, I will get it for you," Tessa said.

Before Lydia could stop her she rushed to the top of the stairs and screamed at the top of her small voice:

"Mohammed, Mohammed!"

Lydia heard the answering tones of a man's voice, and then the child said imperiously:

"Bring up the luggage at once! Do you hear? At once!"

She came back into the room. "He will bring it up now," she announced.

42

"Don't you think you ought to have said 'please'?" Lydia suggested.

She felt this somewhat precocious child could do with being rebuked.

"They are only natives," Tessa answered. "Mummy says they are like animals and the more you beat them the better they work."

"Well, that certainly isn't true of animals," Lydia said almost hotly.

Then she checked herself, feeling she was being rather absurd in arguing with a child.

Tessa, quite unabashed, had sat down on her bed and was regarding her with wide eyes.

"You know, you aren't going to like it here," she said.

"Why ever not?" Lydia asked, surprised.

"You won't!" Tessa said slowly. "You won't like us a bit, and Mummy won't like you, anyway; you're too pretty!"

Lydia felt this was beyond her. She had nothing to say to this incredible child, and with a sigh of relief she heard Ann's voice and saw her outside on the landing.

"I have come up, Ann," she called, "to wash and change. I am too dirty to face a party."

"Oh, I am going down again," Ann replied. "It looked rather fun to me. Why, who's this?" she asked as she caught sight of Tessa.

"My name is Tessa," the child answered, " and Mummy and I live here for the moment."

"You do, do you!" said Ann, "and who may Mummy be?"

Lydia had longed to ask the same question.

"My Mummy is Lady Higley," Tessa answered bluntly, "and she has divorced my Daddy, and so we just go about living wherever we want to."

She said the last words defiantly, then added in a sorrowful little voice with a childish droop of the mouth:

"It's not much fun, really."

Lydia felt for the first time that she was, after all, only a child.

Ann looked at Lydia and raised her eyebrows.

"Mother would like to see you," she said, "if you will go into her. I am going downstairs."

"I am going too," Tessa said.

"Isn't it your bedtime?" Lydia asked.

"My bedtime's when I am tired," Tessa answered, "not before!"

Jumping down from the bed she smoothed down her abbreviated frock before she scampered down the stairs in front of Ann, defiant but with a kind of elfish charm which made Lydia like her in spite of her precociousness.

Alone, Lydia pulled off her hat and, looking at herself in the mirror, smoothed down the dark waves of her hair against her forehead. She smiled at the memory of Tessa's words:

"Mummy won't like you—you're too pretty!"

Already she knew that she disliked Lady Higley—it was instinctive; then she chided herself for making an impulsive decision and for being too critical. But she knew Nina Higley was the type of woman with whom she would never have anything in common, however charitable her inclination.

When she had washed her hands, Lydia turned towards Mrs. Carlton's door. Before knocking, she hesitated a moment, a little fearful, a little apprehensive of what Ann's mother would be like.

Then she turned the handle of the door as a low voice said: "Come in!"

The shutters were closed and the room was half in darkness, so that Lydia's first impressions were of a vast cool space, of white curtains, and the soft carpet into which her feet sank. She looked about her, bewildered.

She saw her at last, lying on a sofa before the far window, a white ermine rug covering her legs and her head laid back against pastel-shaded silk curtains. Lydia closed the door behind her and walked across the room.

As she drew near Margaret Carlton held out a thin hand towards her and said: "Welcome to Egypt."

Lydia took the outstretched hand, and looking down into the pale face of her hostess, felt a sharp surprise.

She had expected something so different, someone still beautiful, someone whose appearance was consistent with her history of passionate romance.

'Why, she's old,' Lydia thought. 'Old, lined and . . . unattractive!'

44

CHAPTER SIX

Lydia looked at the white face, listened to the low, somewhat plaintive voice which asked her questions about Evelyn and the journey and found her thoughts returning continually to Gerald Carlton.

'He is young,' she thought, 'young and attractive; this woman is old. What can he feel for her except pity?'

Talking to Margaret, she tried to discover some charm in her, some fascination, even some quality which made for friendship, but without avail.

As soon as her eyes grew accustomed to the dim light, she noticed that there was a carelessness about her which was quite unnecessary though she were an invalid.

Her clothes were not well kept; her hair needed brushing and arranging, and the powder was carelessly dabbed on her face.

'Perhaps she feels really ill,' Lydia thought, but that would not bridge the disparity of age between husband and wife.

"You have seen Gerald—my husband?" Margaret asked, after Lydia had finished her account of the journey.

"Yes, but only for a few minutes. He has a big party downstairs to look after."

"Gerald likes parties," Margaret said; "and I used to enjoy them once, but now they make my head ache. Nothing is much use now to me."

Lydia felt embarrassed; Margaret had spoken in a tone of bitter rebellion, and she wondered how to offer sympathy or what to say.

"I am so sorry for you," she murmured at last, speaking gently.

"I shall never get used to being like this," Margaret answered. "If you only knew, Mrs. Bryant, what it is like to lie here day after day, week after week, year after year, knowing that I can never get up again, never wear nice clothes, never have any fun."

She paused, but Lydia was silent at this sudden outburst of unhappiness.

"And when I see my daughter," Margaret went on, "when I see Ann looking so much like I was before this happened—"

She broke off, a sob in her voice, tears welling into her eyes. Lydia knew then what had upset her—the sight of Ann, lovely, young, and radiant.

She put out her hand and took Margaret's, trying without words to convey her sympathy and understanding.

"Everyone thought I was beautiful," Margaret said, "and I was. It is not conceited of me to say that. I will show you a photograph so that you can see for yourself."

She spoke feverishly now and rang the bell by her side.

Almost instantly, as if someone had been expecting the summons, the door at the extreme end of the room opened and a nurse stood in the doorway.

"Bring me my photograph books, Dandy," Mrs. Carlton commanded. "All of them—quickly."

The nurse, instead of obeying her order, however, came farther into the room.

"Now, now," she said soothingly, "you are exciting yourself, you know you are. You shall have the photograph books, my dear, but all in good time."

"Oh, Dandy, don't be so irritating," Margaret answered in the tones of a fretful child. "I want Mrs. Bryant to see them now."

Lydia smiled at the nurse.

"Good evening," she said, "I would love to see them sometime, but perhaps we had better wait until tomorrow."

"Oh, you'd better have them," Nurse answered, her eyes on her patient; "she will fret if she doesn't get her own way. We all spoil you, don't we, dear?"

She moved Margaret's pillows and raised her a little in the bed and Lydia could see that there was affection and understanding between nurse and patient.

To look at, Nurse was not of the conventional type. She

46

was fat, with a round jolly face which might in her youth have been attractive, and she had luxuriant dark hair showing in tight curls beneath her starched cap.

When she laughed her face creased into a myriad of wrinkles, her eyes twinkled between dark eyelashes, and two dimples showed in her fat cheeks. She switched on the lights, but when Margaret suggested that she would rather have the shutters open, she said:

"No, it will be getting dark soon, and you know it makes you miserable looking out at the twilight and feeling romantic. We'll be cosy with the lights on and you can show your photograph books and have a good cry!"

"Don't be so beastly to me, Dandy!" Margaret answered. "You know perfectly well I never cry over my photograph books, and I want Mrs. Bryant to see them because she comes from home—Evelyn Marshall sent her to us. You have heard me talk of Evelyn, haven't you?"

"Often enough," Nurse answered.

Pulling open a drawer she found the books and brought them to the side of the sofa.

The next half-hour was spent in turning over the pages while Margaret explained every photograph to Lydia, telling her again and again how lovely she was, and what a good time she had had.

'Does she live entirely in the past,' Lydia asked herself? 'She has got so much in spite of her infirmities. A husband, money, friends, and now a daughter to interest her.'

But it was only of the days when she rode, danced, and was lovely, admired by every man she met, that Margaret talked.

Even the numerous photographs of her in Egypt and in other parts of the world were but a record of amatory conquests.

"That is Colonel Braithwaite," she said pointing to the usual indistinct snapshot of a man in tennis flannels. "He was madly in love with me all one summer. Gerald was terribly jealous and we had awful scenes about him.

"The man on a horse is Lord Starton. He sent me masses of flowers after dancing only once with me. His wife was furious, especially as she had already refused to meet me because Gerald and I were living in sin."

Margaret showed no embarrassment in referring to the

47

years she had spent with Gerald, undivorced from Sir John and an outcast from respectable society.

The photographs ended abruptly with a picture of herself mounted on a big chestnut mare.

"That is the horse that threw me!" she said in a low, bitter tone and shut the book with a bang.

"There are no more photographs!" she added, "and there never will be."

"Thank you for showing me your books," Lydia said.

Then, anxious to change the subject, to chase away the pain and suffering on that pale face, she went on:

"I think your house is terribly attractive, Mrs. Carlton, and I am longing to see the garden tomorrow."

Mrs. Carlton shrugged her shoulders.

"I am not very interested in it, but my husband likes it. We haven't been here long. We lived farther out by Mena House until about two years ago and then he thought it more convenient—it is, for his parties, at any rate."

'Is she jealous of her husband's friends?' Lydia wondered, and remembering Lady Higley, she thought it more than likely.

Nurse brought an end to the conversation by saying it was time that she got Margaret ready for dinner, and Lydia left the room with a sense of relief.

It had been an unexpectedly difficult interview, and while she was sorry for her hostess, she could not help feeling that Margaret was making little effort to fill her life with anything save regrets.

It was desperately hard for her being crippled, yet thinking only of the past and bewailing her lost youth was not going to make the years pass quicker or more easily.

When Lydia got back to her room she unpacked, and finding no one about to help her found her own way to the bathroom.

By the time she had bathed and changed into a simple evening dress, it was nearly half-past eight, but Ann had not come up to dress for dinner and Lydia hesitated to go down again feeling a little uncertain of what was expected of her.

Finally, when she was wondering whether to ring the

bell and ask a servant what time they had dinner, Ann came upstairs with Lady Higley.

"Oh, you have changed!" Nina Higley said, seeing Lydia at the door of her room. "You needn't have troubled. The last of them has only just gone and we will have dinner as soon as it is ready."

"But I must have a bath," Ann cried. "I am filthy after travelling. Don't wait for me. I will be as quick as I can."

"All right," Lady Higley answered her.

Turning to Lydia she said:

"If you want Mr. Carlton you will find him in the drawing room."

There was an insolent note in her voice, but Lydia with a quiet "thank you," went slowly down the stairs.

As she opened the door of the drawing-room she heard Gerald Carlton cursing one of the servants who had dropped several of the glasses which were being cleared away.

He was speaking with a vehemence which was quite out of proportion to the magnitude of the accident, and Lydia hesitated in the doorway. She was just about to retreat when he turned and saw her.

"Come in," he said. "This damn' fool has smashed half my new set of glasses. Heavens, how I loathe native servants!"

His face was flushed and Lydia realized that he had drunk too many cocktails.

"What a nuisance," she said slowly. "But it is always rather unwise to use good glasses for a cocktail party. Don't you think so?"

"It certainly is here," Gerald answered. "Nothing remains unbroken for more than a month at any rate."

He moved towards the open windows.

"Come into the garden," he said. "I am angry, I need the cool air."

Lydia followed. Outside it was dark. Against the starstrewn sky the high palms were silhouetted. For some moments they walked in silence over the grass.

The air was cool and fragrant with the scent of flowers; the lights of the town glittered in the distance. Lydia did not speak and it was Gerald who finally broke the silence.

"Have you seen my wife?" he asked.

"I was with her a long time," Lydia answered, "in fact, until Nurse turned me out so that she could get her ready for dinner."

"Dandy's a splendid person," Gerald said.

There was a silence which was unbroken until Nina Higley called to them from the verandah that dinner was ready.

They walked back together towards the house and Lydia had the feeling that Gerald had been shy and unusually reserved.

He had asked her no questions about England, and while she felt it would have been tactless to start a conversation, unless she were quite certain that he wished to speak of all that he had left behind so many years ago, she had a strong impression that it had been an effort for him to remain silent.

Nina Higley had not changed her dress—she had only made up her face a little more vividly than before, but when Ann came down a few moments later, dressed in a soft rest-gown, she said ill-naturedly:

"I feel very plain amongst all these birds of paradise. We shall have to look to our manners, you and I, Gerald, now we have such smart people in the house."

Gerald, however, took no notice of her remarks.

He talked to Ann the whole way through dinner, telling her what amusements she would find in Cairo and making plans for her entertainment on the morrow.

"I'll tell you who you must ask here," Ann said, "a very nice man who looked after us on the ship. We met him in Paris—Harold Taylor."

Nina Higley gave a little scream.

"Not Hard-Hearted Harry," she said, "he's a distant cousin of mine and the biggest bore on earth. He has never been known to look at a woman, so don't tell me that he has fallen for you. I can't bear it."

"I wasn't a success with him," Ann replied mischievously, "but Lydia was, he never left her side on the boat, always tucking her into her rug and looking after her."

"Don't be ridiculous!" Lydia answered.

But she knew that Nina Higley gave her a look which was far from friendly. A chaperone should not be attractive.

"I have met him several times," Gerald said. "Of course he must come to a meal, especially if he's Mrs. Bryant's young man!"

"He's nothing of the sort," Lydia said cooly. "Ann is merely being ridiculous and I am sure Major Taylor would be horrified if he thought we were talking about him like this."

"I never could stick him myself," Nina said. "Actually, he's a relation of my husband's—not mine, and there is no love lost between us, I can tell you. If he comes here I shall go out, I promise you that."

This, Lydia thought, was perhaps the explanation of Harold Taylor's veiled hints that she might not be entirely happy in the Carlton household. He must have known that Lady Higley and her child were living with Ann's mother and stepfather.

But she was annoyed that Ann should have given a wrong impression of the relationship between Harold Taylor and herself, and to change the subject she asked after Tessa.

"Has she gone to bed?" she inquired.

"I expect so," Nina Higley replied, "she is not allowed down to dinner at any rate. Goodness knows I have enough trouble with the child as it is. If only I could find a good, reliable nurse I should be thankful."

"Is it six you have had in two months?" Gerald asked with a smile.

"But they were all impossible," Nina replied. "Objected to everything I wanted them to do and made the child rather more obnoxious than she is already."

"But who looks after her now?" Lydia asked.

"Anyone who has the time to spare," was the reply; "even Gerald has taken his turn."

"I don't think she likes me much," Gerald said ruefully. Nina gave her high metallic laugh.

"Poor boy; is there one female in the world who doesn't fall for your charms?"

"Apparently," Gerald answered, while Ann, catching Lydia's eye across the table, made a little grimace.

Later when they went up to bed Ann came into Lydia's room.

"Isn't she ghastly?" she asked, sitting down on the bed.

51

"Who?" Lydia asked, but knowing well to whom Ann referred.

"Nina Higley, of course," Ann replied. "I think she is one of the most poisonous women I have ever met. I like Gerald—I can't think why he cares for her."

"How do you know he does? It may be kindness having her here," Lydia suggested, "but I am very sorry for the child."

"Oh, she's a spoiled little beast!" Ann answered, "and as for Gerald being kind—one or two people at the party informed me that she was 'Gerald's latest'."

"Ann, how awful," Lydia said. "What did you say?"

"Oh, they didn't know who I was," Ann explained. "You know nobody ever gets introduced and there was such a crowd there, so I just passed it off with a laugh and asked who was her predecessor."

Lydia looked scandalized.

"But those people will realize who you are later," she said, "and be horrified at what they have said to you."

"It won't matter," Ann said, "they will have said it to so many people by then that they won't be sure it was me."

"Anyway," Lydia answered, remembering her role as Ann's chaperone, "I don't think you ought to believe stories about your stepfather until you know him better."

"My dear," Ann said, "are you surprised if he does have flirtations? I think it is absolutely marvellous the way he has stuck to my mother, anyway."

"Ann!" Lydia exclaimed. "What an awful thing to say."

"Well, why not say it?" Ann asked, "if I think it; and of course I think it, and so do you if you are honest. Why, mother is years older than him, and you have only to look at her to know that what I'm saying is true."

Lydia was silent. Ann got off the bed and walked towards the open window. She looked out; then, after a moment, and in quite a different voice, she said:

"I am glad to-day's over."

"Why?" Lydia questioned.

"I was nervous," Ann said, "nervous and, I suppose, a little afraid of seeing my mother. I had hated her so all these years."

"Hated her?" Lydia asked.

"Because she left me," Ann explained. "Oh, I know, a

child of seven isn't supposed to understand much, but I knew what had happened; the servants talked. They said things about her which have always remained in my memory, and I cannot forget them even if I try, and when I learnt, as I grew older, that I was not to be allowed to see her, I loathed her.

"It was a kind of jealousy, I suppose—a desire to be more important to her than the man she had run away with.

"I was fond of my father in a sort of way, and I think he was fond of me, but he never showed his affection, and I needed affection, longed for someone to make a fuss of me—I expect I am like my mother in that respect.

"Always at the back of my mind was the hurt of her leaving me—I was her child, her only child, and she could leave me behind without a thought.

"I used to lie awake planning how I would get even with her; how I would show her that I didn't care; hurt her, too, in some way or another, and then when I saw her to-day I realized how useless it has all been. A lot of wasted emotion over a woman who means nothing to me nor I to her."

"Oh, Ann, don't be hard," Lydia cried. "I had no idea that it meant so much to you, but don't let that spoil things now. She is so sad, so pathetic, and you can make life so much easier and so much happier for her if you would only try."

"I have a very strong instinct about some things," Ann answered, "and I know with absolute certainty that my mother and I can never mean anything to each other . . . not now."

She didn't say any more but turned around, kissed Lydia lightly, and went from the room.

Alone, Lydia undressed slowly, thinking of the events of the day; of Ann, her mother, and of this strange household to which she had come; she walked out on to the little verandah and stood overlooking the garden.

Everything was silent and still, and suddenly Lydia felt thrilled and excited. The mystery of an Eastern night gripped her and she felt she was on the threshold of new knowledge, a revelation of the eternal truth.

The superficial veil of earthly things was drawn aside;

53

all the petty troubles, worries, difficulties, and misunderstandings of the people with whom she was making her life seemed unimportant. She was one with the Universe, united with the Source of all that was real.

For one perfect moment she saw the plan and pattern of Creation, of which she was a part. She felt a new person, baptized, as it were, by the beauty and the magic of the darkness pierced only by the stars.

How long she stood there she did not know, but she knew she had been vouchsafed a glimpse of all that was best and truest within herself. She was drawn back to earth by the sound of a high metallic laugh.

She started, wrapped her dressing-gown around her, and turned to go back into her bedroom.

She glanced over the balcony to where a shaft of light revealed a part of the verandah and shone on to two people coming down the steps looking at each other.

Then Lydia saw Nina raise her arms and put them around Gerald's neck.

With a shudder of one who has viewed something unclean, Lydia moved back into her bedroom and closed the shutters with a decisive bang.

CHAPTER SEVEN

"But why does Italy look like a boot?" Tessa asked, studying the map in front of her intently.

"I don't know," Lydia answered. "But it does look like one, and Sicily's the ball it is just going to kick."

"I do wish all countries were made like that," Tessa said, "and then it would be terribly easy to remember them. If England was a hand and France two legs dancing, I should never forget them and you'd be awfully pleased with me, wouldn't you?"

"I am very pleased anyway to-day," Lydia said; "you are getting along well."

"Am I really?" Tessa asked a little wistfully.

"Really," Lydia answered.

Tessa suddenly put a warm arm around Lydia's neck and kissed her.

"I do like you," she said; "you are the nicest person I have ever known."

"I am glad," Lydia answered, "and I enjoy teaching you—especially when you try."

"I always try," Tessa said stoutly.

"Not quite always," Lydia corrected, "but generally."

Tessa gave her a smile and climbed down from the table.

"I am going to get ready now," she said, "because Uncle Harold will be here at any moment."

"You mustn't keep him waiting."

"I am not going to," Tessa called, already half-out of the room.

She was like a bit of quicksilver, and Lydia heard her rush through the hall and scamper up the stairs towards her bedroom to change into her riding clothes.

It was only two weeks since Lydia had come to Cairo but already she had one firm friend in the Carlton household in the person of Tessa.

In the contradictory way that spoiled children will attach themselves and show deep affection for the one person who does not spoil them, Tessa had chosen Lydia as a friend and confidante and would do anything that she asked of her.

The person she liked best after Lydia was Major Taylor. He had come to the house to see Lydia, and she had confided in him how sorry she was for Nina Higley's child, without a nurse, without education, and without attention of any sort, and Major Taylor had taken it upon himself to teach Tessa to ride.

Lydia, in the meanwhile, had suggested to Lady Higley that unless Ann wanted her she could spend at least an hour and a half every morning giving Tessa some lessons.

"If it amuses you, do what you like with the child," Nina had replied, "but don't be surprised if she throws the lesson books at your head and don't come complaining to me."

"I won't," Lydia promised.

With a shrug of her shoulders Nina Higley had dismissed the whole matter from her mind and returned to the pursuit of her own amusement and entertainment.

Beginning to know Lady Higley after two weeks in the same house, Lydia had come to the conclusion that no more unsuitable person could possibly have been chosen by Nature to be a mother.

Tessa was often left alone the whole day until it suddenly suited her mother to play a maternal role. When this occurred, Tessa would be taken to party after party, filled with unsuitable food, and kept up until all hours of the night.

The only clothes that were bought for the child were party frocks, while her underclothes were in a disgraceful state, and things like vests and nightgowns, generally too small to be practicable, were left unmended and often unwashed.

Lydia could not bear to see any child brought up in such a state and she found herself attending to Tessa at every available moment.

It was lucky that she had plenty of time on her hands. Ann was immediately swept into a whirl of gaiety, and Lydia was pleased to find that some of the more important people in Cairo who did not bother about Mr. and Mrs. Carlton, were offering hospitality to Ann.

She had found that the morals of the men and women who came to the Carltons' house were best not inquired into.

It had not taken her long to realize that they were by no means the most desirable society for Ann; Gerald's friends, in fact, were the riff-raff of Cairo.

The respectable people were either not asked or would not come.

There were jockeys and trainers; there were young women of doubtful antecedents; there were married couples who had either been divorced several times, or else were just about to be.

There were young men who seemed to have no aim and object in life but to drift about from gay city to gay city spending either their own money in riotous living or somebody else's.

The more Lydia saw of these people the more she wondered at Gerald Carlton.

He certainly appeared to find amusement and entertainment in such company, but when she thought of his home and of Evelyn's description of his parents, she could not reconcile two such extremes.

Cocktail, luncheon, and supper parties were held day after day, and almost every night Lydia would hear her host return late—often when the dawn was already breaking.

She would listen to him coming slowly and unsteadily up the stairs, and knew he was the worse for drink.

He drank heavily, but it seemed to have little effect on him, for the following day he would normally be up before anyone else in the household, riding or motoring off to the Club for a swim.

Lydia liked him, yet she was conscious that he held himself aloof from her.

He was polite and invariably courteous, but he treated her in an entirely different way to the other members of the household.

To everyone else she was already 'Lydia', but Gerald Carlton still used the formal 'Mrs. Bryant' when speaking to her, and she fancied that he deliberately avoided any *tête-à-tête* with her.

She spent two or three hours of every day with Margaret Carlton and grew genuinely sorry for the poor woman. There was little anyone could do for her.

She found it difficult to concentrate for very long on any subject except herself and that inevitably led to bitterness.

Ann's instinct had been right and Lydia knew that Margaret could not bear the sight of her daughter. It irritated and upset her to see the girl come into her sickroom, full of health and vitality, and after a time Ann's daily visits were dropped.

Although Lydia asked no questions she guessed that Ann sensed her mother's feelings and thought it better to keep away.

Dandy, the nurse, was invaluable to the invalid. Her real name was Danton, but she was called 'Dandy' as a term of affection and because in spite of her bulk and age she loved dressing herself up, when off duty, in surprisingly modish and fashionable clothes.

One afternoon, when Margaret was asleep, Dandy joined her in the garden, and they sat under the shade of the flowering trees sewing.

It was nearly tea-time and they heard the sound of a car coming down the drive, and saw Ann sitting beside a dark, handsome man with noticeably white teeth.

"That's Baron Sébale, isn't it?" Lydia asked.

Nurse Danton nodded.

"I shouldn't let the child see too much of him," she said.

"Any particular reason?" Lydia asked.

"A wife is quite a good one, to start with," Dandy replied.

"I hadn't realized he was married," Lydia exclaimed, and she felt anxious, for on several occasions lately the Baron had been in attendance on Ann.

It was difficult for her to remonstrate about any of Ann's new acquaintances. Having met most of them in her stepfather's house, Ann had a ready-made answer to anything Lydia might say about them.

She could not very well tell Ann that she considered that the majority of Gerald Carlton's friends were undesirable, particularly to come in contact with anyone so young and fresh as Ann herself.

She had thought that the Baron, the few times she had noticed him, had seemed better than many other guests in the house. He was invariably sober, unlike most of the men at the end of a cocktail or dinner party.

He had charming manners, and was, she thought, looking at him critically, handsome, especially to a young girl's eyes. But there was something she did not like about him, although for the moment she could not formulate her feeling into anything more than instinct.

Ann waved to the two women sitting under the trees and, followed by the Baron, disappeared into the house.

"What else do you know about him?" Lydia said to Dandy.

"I have heard a great many things that are true, and a great many which might be," Dandy answered slowly. "His father was French, and his mother an Egyptian."

"Egyptian!" Lydia echoed in surprise.

"Yes, his father was a gay old man with a great deal of money and no morals. He kept a kind of harem here in Cairo for years before he died. One of the inmates bore him a son, and he married her so as to legitimize the child. He has been brought up and educated, I believe entirely by English tutors.

"I have met him here for several years now, and in spite of his good manners there is something about him which makes me creep. I don't like him, and I don't want the child to like him too much."

"But his wife?" Lydia asked. "We never see her."

"He married a French girl," Dandy went on; "she left him a week after they were married. There were all sorts of stories and tales as to what she suffered, and how she fled horror-stricken back to her family.

"Whether they were true, I don't know, but she is a Roman Catholic, so she won't divorce him, although I don't think that a lack of freedom worries the Baron very much."

Lydia sat still, frightened at what she had heard.

"What can I do?" she asked, at last, fighting an impulse to get up there and then and go into the house to find Ann and warn her.

"From what I have seen of Ann," Dandy said, "you will have to be very careful and very tactful. She is like her mother. If she gets the bit between her teeth she might bolt."

Lydia got slowly to her feet.

"I think it is tea-time," she said. "I will go in and see if it is ready."

She walked up the verandah steps and into the house by the wide drawing-room windows. When she entered the room two people who had been talking eagerly together a moment before became silent, and stared at her as if she were an interloper.

"I came to see if tea was ready," Lydia explained. "Would you like it here, Ann, or out in the garden?"

"Oh, do let's go out," Ann said to the Baron, turning eagerly towards him and inferring all too obviously that she wished the two of them to be alone.

"But of course," he acquiesced; "we'll run over to the Club, my car is outside."

He smiled at her in a caressing way which made Lydia understand exactly what Dandy had meant when she said he gave her the creeps.

Lydia had tea with Dandy; when it was finished she went upstairs and talked to Margaret Carlton until it was dinnertime.

But while she chatted her thoughts were elsewhere, thinking of Ann, wondering what she was doing, and planning how best she could approach the girl and suggest that she saw less of the Baron.

Ann came back when it was nearly dinner-time, and had to dress in a hurry. There was a look of shining radiance about her as if someone had lit a candle within her.

'She is so young and lovely,' Lydia thought to herself, and her heart sank.

For a change there were no guests for dinner. Lady Higley had been out late the night before, and was not feeling well, so that she had a tray sent up to her room. There were only the three, Gerald, Lydia and Ann.

Ann said very little, but she looked so attractive that Gerald remarked on it, and said that the Cairo air must be doing her good.

Had Nina been present she would, no doubt, have made some sarcastic remark, but Lydia said nothing, and Ann merely smiled happily as though she agreed. She ate very little, and almost as soon as the meal was finished said she was going to bed.

"Then you will have to talk to me, Mrs. Bryant," Gerald said; "no one else seems to wish for my company tonight."

He took another brandy, picked up a large cigar, and strolled from the dining-room on to the verandah.

"Come and sit down," he said, pointing to one of the big wicker arm-chairs filled with cushions, "and tell me the story of your life."

He spoke with a slightly mock___ air, yet Lydia felt that in some extraordinary way he was embarrassed by this *tête-à-tête* which had not been of his seeking.

Ann's bedroom, like her mother's, looked out on to another side of the house; only Lydia's was above the verandah, and she knew that there was no chance of their being overheard.

'Shall I tell him about Ann?' she thought. 'I can't take the responsibility of this all by myself.'

But before she could begin to speak Gerald rose to his feet and said restlessly:

"Let's walk down to the river's edge, it's hot here."

They moved slowly over the green lawn towards the wide path which, bordered by flowering shrubs, led them to where, in the distance, the waters of the Nile shimmered silver under the rising moon.

Lydia's dress of heavy white crêpe made her look like a ghost as she moved silently beside her host.

Suddenly, quite unexpectedly, he asked:

"Why did you come here?"

"Evelyn Marshall suggested that Ann wanted a chaperone and that I might fill the role," Lydia said, in surprise. "Didn't you know?"

"But why did you accept?"

"I wanted a job. I have no money now."

"You have never worked before?" Gerald asked.

Lydia shook her head.

"My husband has only just died," she said; "until he died there was no need for me to work."

"Do you miss him?" Gerald asked this last question less abruptly, and with interest, as though he genuinely wanted to know the answer.

"I hadn't seen him for several years," Lydia replied. "He was ill . . . in fact, he was in a mental home."

They reached the end of the path and stood on the banks of the river. With a sudden gesture Gerald chucked away his cigar, throwing it out into the water. Its glowing end was quenched as it fell.

"You still haven't answered my question," he said. "Why have you come here?"

"I am afraid I don't understand," Lydia said. "I have told you."

She spoke abruptly, for Gerald, turning towards her, suddenly seized her in his arms, holding her fiercely against him, pressing his lips to hers. For a moment Lydia was too surprised, too startled, then, as suddenly as he had held her, he let her go."

"How dare you!" she said. "How dare you touch me!"

"Are you surprised?" Gerald asked, putting his hands on her shoulders. He held her, looking down at her. "Are you surprised, when you come here looking like all the things that I have forgotten, or that I have tried to forget? God, I wish I had never set eyes on you!"

Roughly he moved her aside, and without another word walked swiftly back the way they had come, leaving Lydia alone.

She stood staring after him, one hand raised to her breast, quelling the tumult which shook her. She was too bewildered at what had occurred to think coherently for a few minutes.

Then gradually the hot blood died away from her cheeks, and she became calmer until only her mouth, bruised from the violence of his kiss, made her overwhelmingly conscious of what had happened.

'He must be mad,' she thought to herself.

But she knew that the expression on his face and in his eyes revealed to her in the light of the moon, had not been that of a madman, but of one driven beyond his strength.

For a long time Lydia stood by the waters of the Nile, and then slowly she walked back to the house.

She went in by the front door, avoiding the open, still-lighted windows of the drawing-room, but as she passed the door she saw that she need not have been afraid of a further encounter with her host.

On one of the tables stood his glass and a half-empty bottle of brandy; the room was empty, and she knew that Gerald had gone out to find amusement, and perhapus forgetfulness.

Upstairs there was a light under Ann's room, and Lydia knocked gently.

"Come in," Ann answered.

She entered to find the girl sitting, still dressed, by the window looking out on to the night.

"I wondered if there was anything I could do for you," Lydia said.

"Nothing," Ann replied. "I was just thinking of going to bed."

She was obviously disinclined to talk, and Lydia, after trying to make conversation for two or three minutes, gave it up, and, wishing her good-night, went to her own room.

She undressed, and wrapping her dressing-gown around her decided to read for a little while before dropping off to sleep. She remembered that she had left her book in Dandy's room, having gone in there after being with Margaret before dinner.

'She won't be asleep,' Lydia thought, 'I will go in and fetch it.'

She opened the door of her room and as she did so had a fleeting glimpse of someone just passing out of sight downstairs. For a moment she hesitated. Although she could not be certain, she felt a sudden instinct that the person had been Ann.

She walked to the top of the landing but she was too late, for there was only the sound of the front door closing.

'It couldn't have been Ann,' Lydia thought to herself.

But to make sure she went to the girl's room and knocked on the door. There was no answer. Determinedly Lydia turned the handle and entered.

The room was empty; the bed unslept in.

That was why she went to bed early, it was merely an excuse to slip out and meet the Baron.

At the far end of the passage there was an empty spare room. It looked down the front drive. Lydia ran towards it and reached the window just in time to see dimly through the trees the strong headlights of a motor-car moving away.

'What am I to do?' she wondered. 'What am I to do?'

Since they had come to Cairo, Lydia had arranged that when Ann went to parties at night she had either to go in her stepfather's car which also brought her back, or she was chaperoned by some older woman in the party.

Ann was only eighteen; girls of her generation were being strictly chaperoned in London, and there was no reason why because they were abroad she should be allowed a greater license.

On several occasions Lydia had herself accompanied her, but naturally she was not asked as often as the girl. She believed that, until now at any rate, Ann had been perfectly honorable and come home either with a party or in the car provided for her.

Lydia felt from her knowledge of Ann that rather than lie and say she was going to a party tonight she had preferred to resort to subterfuge so as to meet the Baron secretly, and without argument.

'They will go and see the Pyramids by moonlight,' Lydia guessed.

She knew that such an idea would appeal to any girl, especially Ann, who at the present was incurably romantic.

Dandy's opinion of the Baron was disquieting. Had he been an unmarried man Lydia would not have felt particularly alarmed, for Ann was sensible and in many ways had already shown that she was capable of looking after herself.

But the Baron was different. Lydia felt that he was not a person to be trusted, especially with someone so lovely and so young as Ann.

Miserably Lydia walked up and down the floor of her small bedroom.

It was hopeless for her to try to sleep or rest until she knew that Ann was safe, and until the girl returned she could only wait and pray that all would be well. She wondered what Evelyn would have done in the circumstances.

Even Evelyn, who was so resourceful, so practical, and invariably sensible under any circumstances, might have been at a loss at this moment and as helpless as she was herself.

She had left her door open and suddenly she heard a scream from Tessa's room. It was farther down the passage. She hurried in to the child and found her sitting up in bed in tears.

"I had a dreadful dream," she sobbed; "a terrible dream, Aunt Lydia."

Lydia put her arms about her and tried to soothe her.

"It is quite all right," she said, "now you are awake and nothing can hurt you, it can't really."

"It was a horrid dream," Tessa said.

"I know," Lydia replied, "but never mind. I expect it was all those prawns you ate for luncheon. You did eat rather a lot, didn't you?"

Tessa smiled suddenly through her tears.

"They were awfully good," she said.

"I know," Lydia answered, "but that is always the trouble. We usually have to pay for what we enjoy in some way or another."

"Am I paying for them by having horrid dreams?" Tessa asked.

"For eating too many," Lydia said. "Your poor tummy couldn't cope with them and so it has given you a pain."

Tessa laughed.

"You do have funny ideas," she said. "But I shan't be frightened again if it is only my poor tummy paying for eating too many prawns!"

"Well, that's all right," Lydia said.

She tucked the child in and bent down to kiss her.

"Aunt Lydia," Tessa asked suddenly, "do you pray to God when you want things?"

"Yes, I do," Lydia answered solemnly.

"Do you always get what you want?" Tessa asked.

"Not always," Lydia said. "Sometimes God doesn't think it is good for us and He knows far better than we do."

"I prayed like anything yesterday when I was out riding," Tessa said. "I prayed that Uncle Harold would say that he could come today and give me another lesson, and he did. It was all right, so God made him, didn't he?"

"I expect He put the idea into his head," Lydia said gently.

"I would rather ride than do anything in the world," Tessa said, "especially with Uncle Harold."

"You mustn't be disappointed if he can't come every day—he's a very busy man, you know."

"I love him very much," Tessa said. "More than anyone in the world except you, I think; but Mummy hates him, she told me so."

"I don't think she meant that, Tessa," Lydia answered, "so I shouldn't think about it. People often say lots of things they don't mean, you know."

"It is funny Mummy should dislike Uncle Harold when I like him so much, Tessa said, "because she generally likes men whoever they are. But then Uncle Harold is not her sort, is he?"

Lydia debated with herself as to whether she could give Tessa a lecture on loyalty and then decided it was too late tonight. Instead, she knelt down beside the bed and said:

"Don't think about it now, darling. Just go to sleep and we'll talk in the morning instead, shall we?"

Tessa gave her a quick hug.

"I do love you, dear Aunt Lydia," she whispered, "and you are the prettiest person in the world."

Lydia got to her feet laughing.

"You are a flatterer," she said. "Good night, my poppet, sleep well."

She closed the door gently behind her. There was a warm glow in her heart as she walked back to her own room. At last someone in this household was very lovable.

There was so much that was sweet about Tessa, and Lydia thought for the thousandth time that it was a crime that she should be brought up the way she was.

Had she not been there the child would merely have cried herself to sleep again with no one within call. Lady Higley had purposely arranged that her child was put the other side of the house from her room.

Nina Higley had been particularly ungracious at Lydia's

and Harold Taylor's efforts to do something for Tessa.

It was Lydia who had suggested the child should call grown-ups 'Uncle' and 'Aunt' rather than speak to them familiarly.

Nina Higley's comment on this innovation was characteristic of the woman.

"A very peculiar lot of new relations I seem to have acquired," she said sarcastically, and added in Tessa's hearing: "How thrilled Hard-Hearted Harry must be by this new intimacy between us."

Lydia had already learned that it was usless to argue or even try and explain things to Lady Higley. She put her own egotistical and selfish interpretation on everything, however kindly or disinterestedly a person's actions might be.

Back in her own bedroom Lydia found it was eleven o'clock. She sat down in an arm-chair to wait, and then remembered she had not yet got her book. But it was too late to disturb Dandy now.

She went downstairs to the drawing-room. From the bookcase she chose a light novel which she felt might help her to pass the hours away.

She had turned towards the door to return to her room when the sound of the front door opening startled her.

'Perhaps it is Ann,' she hoped, but a moment later she knew she was mistaken.

It was Gerald who had returned home.

CHAPTER EIGHT

Gerald flung down his hat on the hall table, turned towards the drawing-room and saw Lydia standing in the doorway.

She noticed that he was breathing heavily as though he had walked fast and that his patent-leather shoes were covered with dust.

They stood looking at each other in the bright lights, Lydia a little pale, one hand clutching her pale-pink dressing-gown round her, the other holding the novel.

"I came down for a book," she said lamely at last.

There was an embarrassed silence between them and then she added courageously:

"I also wanted to talk to you."

"Now?" he asked.

"Ann has gone out—alone," Lydia replied.

She saw that he did not understand. For all he knew, Ann might have gone to a party or be out with friends, as she often was.

"I mean," Lydia said, "that she has gone out alone with Baron Sébale, at least I think so. She crept out of her room."

"Wait a minute," Gerald said. "Let's get this straight. Shall we go into the drawing-room? It seems pointless to discuss anything standing here."

Lydia followed him to the wide sofa near the fireplace. She was too anxious about Ann, too relieved that at last she had a chance of telling someone about it, to worry as to what she looked like.

She sat down primly on the edge of the sofa, wrapping the dressing-gown still farther around her.

"Why should you think she is with the Baron?" Gerald asked.

"I think she is beginning to fall in love with him," Lydia answered, "they have been together a lot lately. He met her at luncheon today and afterwards brought her back here. They went to the Club for tea, at least that's where they said they were going, and Ann didn't return until nearly dinner-time. You remember that after we finished dinner she said she was going up to bed."

Thinking of what had happened after Ann had gone she faltered a little and felt a deep flush creep into her cheeks, but she forced herself to go on speaking as steadily as she could.

"When I came back to the house," she said, "I went to Ann's room. She didn't seem to want to talk to me, but she had not yet begun to undress. I only stayed with her a few moments as she said she was tired.

"It was about half an hour later that I saw her slipping downstairs and found that her room was empty. There was a car waiting for her at the end of the drive and I can only imagine that it was the Baron she was meeting."

Gerald had listened to her with attention. Now he lit a cigarette, and as he bent his head to the flame Lydia glanced at him.

She could not help thinking that he was attractive, but she was angry with him, she told herself—he had behaved like a cad.

"Aren't you making rather a mountain out of a mole-hill?" he asked at last.

"Ann is eighteen," Lydia answered. "Your friend the Baron is a married man and half-Egyptian."

"So you know about him, do you?" Gerald said; "and why the accent on my friend?"

"Isn't he your friend?" Lydia asked.

"He comes here a good deal. You think he is my friend yet you don't consider him a desirable acquaintance for my stepdaughter?"

"Of course I don't!" Lydia said hotly; his attitude was beginning to make her annoyed.

"And why is he so undesirable?" Gerald asked.

"To begin with, he is a married man," Lydia answered.

"Aren't you being somewhat old fashioned?"

Lydia rose to her feet.

"At least I expected some help from you," she said. "I see I was wrong. I will go to Ann's mother."

"I don't think she will be able to help you," Gerald answered, "and I am sure she will be loyal enough not to label my friends as undesirable. Is the Baron your only *bête noire,* or have you any others?"

Lydia had no thought of caution or politeness.

"I am afraid," she said, "I consider most of the people Ann meets here most undesirable. They are not fit acquaintances in any way for a young girl, who has not yet seen the world."

She took a deep breath and continued:

"You may like to associate with bookmakers, jockeys, and men like Baron Sébale—I don't, and I considered it part of my duty when I came here to prevent Ann from knowing such people. Apparently I was wrong."

"You prefer her only to know those people who have gone out of their way, in the past, to be offensive to her mother?" Gerald retorted.

Lydia started. This was a point of view she had not considered.

"But if you think those are the people I am going to entertain in this house, you are much mistaken," Gerald went on. "The men and women that you consider undesirable were my friends in difficult times, they shall remain so now, and your so-called respectable society can do what they like; they shan't at any rate enjoy my hospitality."

He spoke angrily, almost shouting the words at her, and Lydia began to understand and realize what was the explanation of much that had troubled her.

He had not forgotten, could never forget, the years when he and the woman he loved had been social outcasts. He resented the slights they had endured, the scandal which had been caused by his elopement.

He was bitter and revengeful, and he filled his house now with the people with whom in the years that were past he had been forced to associate.

At last the reason for the strange parties, the forced gaiety, the presence of women like Nina Higley, was plain.

Gerald hated society because it has ostracized him.

He was glorying in his reputation, trying to be worse than in fact he was, and doing all in his power to forget or smother those instincts which, because of his upbringing, were still the strongest and best within him.

Lydia understood, and as she faced him she realized a little of the hell he must have endured through the years that were past.

He was an Englishman who loved England, who had been born and bred in the country, but he was exiled because of his mad infatuation when he was a mere boy of twenty-two.

On the impulse Lydia put out her hand and touched his arm.

"I am so sorry," she said, "I didn't understand."

She turned from him and without another word left the room.

Upstairs she stood for a long time thinking. She saw the years had not only taken toll of Margaret's looks, they had also broken Gerald's pride and humbled him.

She saw how easily Margaret Taverel's beauty had persuaded her young lover that the world was well lost for love. She saw how gradually the realization must have come to both of them that they had been wrong.

Then Margaret's accident had smashed the last link between them, making them two separate suffering people, perhaps hiding their anguish from the world but never from each other.

He was tied to a woman he no longer wanted by unbreakable chains of loyalty; a woman who craved only her lost beauty, not the man who had sacrificed his life for it.

Not even Sir John could have wished for a more complete revenge on his erring wife. No tortures could have added to their retribution.

Gerald was seeking to forget, not the love or misery or suffering, but an old house standing amongst green meadows and carrying within it the joy of his boyhood.

He wanted to forget the pride in his mother's voice, the hand of his father on his shoulder, the servants who had known and loved him since a child.

He could forget only when he drank in the company of raffish people, or when he danced in the hot, fetid air of night clubs.

72

There were tears in Lydia's eyes; slowly they welled on to her cheeks until as she rose to get a handkerchief she realized that she was crying, and crying for Gerald Carlton—the boy he had been and the man he had become.

Suddenly she was afraid, not for him, but for herself.

* * * *

It was nearly one o'clock when Ann finally returned. Lydia heard her coming in. Someone else had been waiting also for Ann. Gerald came out of the drawing-room; she heard him say:

"Where have you been?"

By the door of her bedroom she listened for the answer. Quite clearly the voice came up the stairs.

"I have been out." Ann's tone was defiant.

"Who with?"

There was a pause.

"Do you think you have any right to question me?" Ann asked.

"I think I have, don't you?" Gerald answered.

Ann was obviously nonplussed at this reply.

"Why should you think that?" she asked rather lamely.

"For one thing, this is my house," Gerald answered; "secondly, your mother is not well and therefore cannot be worried; and thirdly, you met the Baron under my roof."

"How do you know I have been with the Baron?" Ann said hotly.

"Well, haven't you?" Gerald insisted, but very quietly. Lydia was surprised at the gentleness of his tone.

"We only went to see the Pyramids," Ann said.

Her voice was less defiant now as though she thought it wiser to be conciliatory.

'I was right,' Lydia thought to herself. 'Of course he is playing on the child's romantic fancies.'

Listening she heard Gerald say:

"We are all tired to-night, and it is hardly a good moment for a long talk, is it? Will you promise that you will give me an opportunity to discuss this with you in the morning?"

"I am riding at nine o'clock," Ann said glumly.

"With him?" Gerald asked.

"Yes!"

"Well then, I will be up at eight o'clock if you will," Gerald said. "We will have breakfast together and talk things out. Is that a promise?"

"I won't swear to be punctual," Ann answered, "but I will do my best."

She came running lightly up the stairs and Lydia only just had time to shut her door.

'My fears have been unfounded,' she thought, 'Ann has come home quite safely, and Gerald, having taken my words to heart, will now persuade his stepdaughter to find more desirable friends. I am a fool to get so worked up.'

She was tired and her head ached after the anxiety and the occurrences of the evening. She slipped off her dressing-gown and got into bed, but a moment later there came a tap on her door.

"Who is there?" she asked apprehensively, wild thoughts coming into her head.

"It is me," came the answer.

Ann came into her room.

"I guessed you were awake," she said. "I saw the light under your door."

She sat down on the end of the bed.

"You told Gerald, didn't you?" she said accusingly. "I thought you must have seen me go."

"I was awfully worried," Lydia answered.

"Why?"

"You know why," Lydia replied. "Oh, Ann, dear, don't think I am being interfering over this, but you are very young and very pretty."

"I can't help it," Ann answered. "He is fascinating, you must admit that."

Lydia pulled the pillows behind her back; she realized that Ann wanted to talk and wondered what she was to say. Ann was in love for the first time. Like all girls of her age, she wanted to discuss with someone her new emotions, her dreams and desires.

"I don't think I admire him." Lydia said cautiously.

"He's half Egyptian," Ann corrected. "Didn't I tell you, Lydia, that I should find some affinity in the land of the Pharaohs? You can't deny that I had a presentiment about it, can you?"

"Are you suggesting that Baron Sébale was part of your last reincarnation?" Lydia asked.

"I can't be sure, of course," Ann answered, angered by the sarcasm in Lydia's tone. "But I can't help feeling it was Fate that I should meet him and that he should be a direct descendant of those who built the Pyramids."

"Did he tell you that?" Lydia asked. "I always understood that his mother was a very ordinary native girl in his father's harem."

"Oh, he told me lots of things about himself," Ann said dreamily.

"And about his wife?" Lydia asked.

"Oh, she was a perfect idiot. She ran away from him. Can you imagine it, actually running away on their honeymoon. He didn't want to marry her, but the marriage was arranged and her parents were awfully keen on it. Of course they were!"

"The Baroness might tell a very different story," Lydia suggested. "Do you think the Baron is the type of person to make a good husband?"

"I wish I could have the opportunity of finding out!"

Lydia felt that this nonsense must be stopped at once.

"Ann, darling," she said, "you mustn't be ridiculous, or have absurd ideas about someone like Baron Sébale. He is a married man, and what possible good can come of your imagining yourself in love with him, or he with you? He can never marry you.

"You know his wife is a Roman Catholic and therefore there is no chance of a divorce. Why not forget him before it is too late? Give him up! Don't see him! There are hundreds of other young men in Cairo."

"Oh, they are all bores," Ann answered with the contempt of youth. "You can't talk me out of being in love, Lydia, however much you try. I adore Ali and I know he worships me. You needn't be afraid of him hurting me in any way. Why, to-night he only kissed my hand and the hem of my dress!"

She said the last words with a tremulous note in her voice and Lydia knew that she had been thrilled and touched by this Oriental theatricalism.

'She is only young,' she thought; 'it's no use talking to her, she is infatuated and not even ashamed to say so.'

With a little sigh, however, she attempted once again to reason with her.

"Since you have been here," she asked, "have you thought of your mother's elopement with your stepfather?"

Ann looked surprised at her question.

"Why?" she asked. "What has that got to do with me?"

"Only this: Gerald was very young when he first took a false step which ruined his life," Lydia replied. "Do you think he is particularly happy?"

"I never thought about it," Ann answered; "but then, of course my mother had that accident, and of course, she is years older than Gerald. She looks it, doesn't she?"

They were getting away from the point that Lydia wanted to make; she tried to keep Ann from side-tracking her.

"I only wanted to show you that I don't believe unconventionality ever pays; it never brings lasting happiness, only misery."

"You are only trying to frighten me," Ann said sharply. "I can't see that there is any parallel between my mother's story and my being in love with Ali. Anyway, I hope I don't ever get to look like her."

"Oh, Ann!" Lydia exclaimed, "what a cruel thing to say."

"She looks awful," Ann said.

She got up from the bed and went towards the mirror. She stared at her own radiant reflection.

"Ali says I am like a star," she said, "a beautiful star in a dark world."

"How dreadfully Ethel M. Dell," Lydia laughed.

"Things always sound like that if you repeat them," Ann answered with a great deal of wisdom. "But they are quite different when they are said to you, and you know it, Lydia."

"Yes, there is a certain amount of truth in that," Lydia answered, trying to be fair, "but to be called a star in a dark world when you are looking at the Pyramids by moonlight with a descendant of the Pharaohs seems to me very like the penny novelettes I used to read under the bedclothes at school."

"I am glad you have actually done things that were

wrong at some time in your life!" Ann said. "You are such a prude that I am quite frightened of you."

She laughed as she spoke and it took the sting from her words. She rose, and putting her arms round Lydia to kiss her good night said as she did so:

"I am so happy!"

When she had gone she left Lydia wakeful and anxious. How could she deal with someone like Ann who took everything in such an inconsequential way, who didn't even mind rebukes, and ignored reprimands? Ann might laugh at her fears but she could not allay them.

'Gerald must speak to the Baron himself,' she thought, but thinking of Gerald brought back vividly to her the moment when he had kissed her.

It was only a few hours ago, so much had happened since then, yet in the darkness she could feel the tenderness of her mouth. His arms too had been so strong.

She felt helpless and impotent, and she knew now that with her surprise and her anger there had been another and strange emotion which she dare not admit even to herself.

CHAPTER NINE

Dandy came into Lydia's room before she was properly awake in the morning.

She pushed open the shutters and drew back the thin cretonne curtains, letting the golden sunshine pour flood-like into the room and throw a blinding beam on to Lydia's eyes.

It seemed to her that she had only just fallen asleep. The events of the night before had kept her awake for a long time after she was undressed and in bed. She had heard the distant clock strike hour after hour.

Finally, when she was resigned to a 'white night,' she had sunk into a dreamless slumber.

"What it is?" she asked sleepily, then yawning and rubbing her eyes as she sat up in bed.

Dandy stood with her hands on her fat hips watching her. With her dark hair tumbled over her white shoulders and with a gentle flush on her cheeks, Lydia looked very young and very attractive as she forced herself to wakefulness.

"I am so sleepy," she said. "You are a nuisance, I could have slept for hours."

"It is nearly eight o'clock," Dandy answered, and with a start Lydia remembered all that had passed the night before and wondered if Ann was getting up ready for her talk with Gerald.

"Is Ann awake?" Lydia asked.

"She is," Dandy answered, "and half-dressed. It is Ann that I came to talk to you about."

Lydia looked at her with a troubled expression on her face, but Dandy laughed.

"It is all right, dearie," she said. "I am not going to add to the difficulties and the troubles you are having with the child. I expected them, and worse, if she came to a house like this. No, it is about her mother. She has had a bad night and I won't have her worried with stories, however important you may think them."

"Then what am I to do?" Lydia asked making as she spoke a little helpless gesture of her hands.

Dandy thought for a moment; then she sat down beside Lydia's bed.

"No amount of talking is going to do any good," she said frankly. "The child has every intention of going her own way, and you know it."

"But, Dandy, don't you see the danger of this man— he's making love to her already, and cleverly, so that she is blinded into thinking him a romantic hero."

"He's stealthy," Dandy said, and Lydia thought how apt the adjective was when applied to the Baron.

"Mr. Carlton is going to speak to Ann this morning," Lydia went on. "Perhaps she will listen to him."

"And if she doesn't?" Dandy asked.

"Then I don't know what to do," Lydia answered. "I had thought of speaking to her mother. You are quite right, Dandy, you guessed it, but if you won't allow me to do that we shall have to think of something else. What about the Baron? Do you think we could tackle him?"

"He wouldn't listen," Dandy said decisively.

"Then what am I to do?" Lydia asked.

"Take her away," Dandy answered, "if she will go."

Lydia sat there thinking, her knees raised under the bedclothes, her face resting in her hands. She thought that perhaps Dandy was pessimistic.

Surely there was a chance that Ann would listen to her stepfather. She liked him, and it was always easier for a man than for a woman to deal with a headstrong girl.

"Oh, dear!" she said at last, "why did Ann have to meet such an awful man? If only he had been an Englishman things would have been so much easier. The people who come to the house are awful, but any one of them would have been easier to deal with than the Baron."

She thought of Gerald's outburst last night and of his bitterness against the society which would not accept him in the years that were past and whom out of spite he would not know now. It seemed such a pity, such a waste of life, money and position.

Not only must he suffer, but through him his step-daughter might be affecting her whole future by becoming entangled with an undesirable friend of his.

"I must get up!" Lydia said, "and I wish you would be more helpful, Dandy."

"My dear, I am an old woman," Dandy answered. "I have learned one lesson in my life and proved it right a thousand times. That is that everyone must buy their own experience."

"But Ann is so pretty and so young," Lydia answered almost pleadingly.

"What does Mrs. Carlton think of the people who come here?" she added suddenly.

"She hardly notices them," Dandy answered. "Can't you see the present means nothing to her? Her spirit lives entirely in the past. She cares for nothing, for nobody."

Dandy's face had softened when she mentioned Margaret, and Lydia, who had seen the care and affection which she lavished on her patient, knew that Margaret's helplessness and unhappiness had made her, in Dandy's eyes, a suffering child to be tended and protected.

But not even love could blind Dandy to the truth—that no-one nowadays be it man, woman or child, could arouse Margaret from her despondency and her egotism.

"But her husband?" Lydia asked, although she knew the answer. "Surely she still loves her husband?"

Dandy shook her head.

"She is jealous only of the women who surround him, not because she wants him, but because their attractions fill her with envy. She wants to be young again, beautiful, able to command admiration, and fascinate not only Gerald Carlton, but every man."

"It is pathetic," Lydia exclaimed.

The two women were interrupted by Tessa, who came into the room with tears in her eyes and a trembling lip, holding out a bleeding finger.

"I fell off a wall," she explained when Lydia asked her what had happened. "I was trying to walk all around the garden without touching the ground. It's a lovely game,

81

but a lizard ran across my toes. It startled me and I fell."

Her finger had been cut deeply by a piece of jagged glass.

Dandy fetched some iodine and bandages. The disinfectant stung Tessa, but she was brave enough to keep her tears from falling though they welled into her eyes.

With all these interruptions, it was nearly nine o'clock by the time she got downstairs, and as she reached the hall she met Ann in her riding-clothes coming out of the dining-room.

"Have you finished breakfast?" Lydia asked. "I am terribly late, but everything seemed to prevent my getting dressed this morning."

"Yes, I have finished," Ann answered. "I am going now. You might give Gerald a message—tell him I couldn't wait for his promised sermon."

"But Ann!" Lydia expostulated quickly, "surely you have seen your stepfather this morning?"

"On the contrary," said Ann with a triumphant smile, "he's not down yet. I am sorry to disappoint you both, but because Gerald doesn't keep appointments, you can't expect me to be late for mine. I am also dining with Ali to-night."

With an air of defiance Ann picked up her riding whip and opened the front door.

Lydia reached out a pleading hand to her, words trembling on her lips, but it was too late. She knew that Ann thought that she and Gerald had conspired together last night.

For her stepfather not to turn up for the arranged conversation between them was, of course, in her view a triumph, and she would not be slow to take advantage of it.

The Baron would be waiting for her and it was now too late to prevent them meeting.

Lydia watched her walk down the steps and into the brilliant sunshine, slender as a young boy, but, in her well-cut jodhpurs and silk shirt, definitely alluring. In her freshness and youth Ann would fire the blood of any man, especially someone like the Baron.

Before she stopped to think, Lydia turned and ran up the stairs towards Gerald's room.

Only as she reached the wide landing did she hesitate for a moment, and as she did so, the door of his room oppened, and Nina Higley, dressed in a pale-blue dressing-gown and carrying a breakfast tray came out.

"Oh, is that you, Mrs. Bryant," she said to Lydia. "Take this, will you, I have finished with it."

There was an insolent note in her voice as though she were speaking to an inferior servant. It was she who had delayed Gerald, and by taking her breakfast with him, he had been unable to see his stepdaughter, probably forgotten all about her.

Without a word, Lydia pushed Lady Higley out of her way, almost roughly, and knocked at the door of the room.

A voice said "Come in."

She entered to see Gerald still in a dressing-gown and pajamas, a cigarette in his hand, come sauntering in to his room from the balcony.

Lydia walked in and slammed the door behind her, shutting out Lady Higley, who was standing in the passage too astonished by her behavior to do anything for the moment.

Furious, her hands clenched, her head thrown back, Lydia faced her host.

"Ann has gone," she said.

"Good God!" Gerald ejaculated. "What's the time? I had no idea it was so late."

"Evidently you had other things to think about," Lydia answered.

"Look here," Gerald said, "has she really gone? I am frightfully sorry but I had honestly forgotten the time."

"You had a chance to do something for Ann," Lydia said; "she went to bed last night prepared to listen to you, but you couldn't trouble to remember her this morning. Heaven knows what she may do now she has time to think, time to discuss things with the Baron. How could you forget? How could you let this happen?"

Gerald put down his cigarette.

"Surely you are attaching an undue importance," he said, "to the fact that I have forgotten an appointment?"

"Perhaps you are right," Lydia answered. "It was absurd to think that you could possibly have any influence with Ann. Your morals and your behavior could hardly be a worse example for her."

She felt she could say no more, her anger was choking her. Without another word she turned and opened the door.

Lady Higley was still outside and Lydia knew that she had been trying to listen to what was being said. She walked past her and into her own bedroom. Only when she was alone did she begin to tremble.

'Losing my temper hasn't done any good,' she thought after a few moments. 'Who cares what I think or say?'

For the first time she began to wonder if Gerald Carlton was in a position to sack her. It was difficult to know to whom she owed her authority.

It was Ann who had engaged her on Evelyn's advice, although the idea of a chaperone had originally come from Margaret.

'I don't care,' Lydia thought, 'I would like to leave and I should do so if it weren't for Ann.

She thought of Nina Higley's astonished face and for the moment wished that she had been really rude to her.

Suddenly she thought of someone whom she could talk to and ask for advice—Harold Taylor. He was sensible and she would not feel with him that she was being disloyal to discuss the members of the household.

She hurried downstairs to the telephone. He was at home.

'I must see you," Lydia said, "could you possibly come now? Not to the house, I will wait for you at the end of the drive if you will pick me up in your car. I must talk to you. I am in trouble."

"I will be there in ten minutes," Harold Taylor answered.

It was characteristic of the man that he wasted no words either in curiosity or sympathy.

With a little sigh Lydia put down the receiver. Someone she could trust, someone she liked, and someone who seemed stable among a crowd of madmen, was coming to her assistance.

She found Tessa and told her to go and play in the garden; there would be no lessons this morning.

"Why not?" Tessa asked despondently. "I want to go on

with our history book, I want to know what happened to the Princes in the Tower. Did they escape? I do hope they did."

"We will do it to-morrow, darling," Lydia promised. "I have to go out now."

"Who with?" Tessa asked.

"With Uncle Harold," Lydia said.

She would have liked to have lied, but knowing that there was every likelihood of Tessa finding out whom she was with, she felt it would undermine her influence with the child were she deceitful.

'Oh, let me come too," Tessa pleaded, but Lydia shook her head.

"Not this morning," she said, "I want to talk to him about something very serious, and that's a secret between you and me; so don't tell the others unless, of course, they ask you."

"They are not likely to ask me," Tessa said. "Nobody ever bothers about me unless I am being a nuisance."

Lydia bent and kissed her. She knew that Lady Higley considered Tessa a nuisance whenever her attention was drawn to the child.

"I won't be long," she said, "and if there is time before luncheon, we'll finish the story of the little Princes in the Tower."

"Oh, lovely!" Tessa said. "Hurry then, because you can come back all the quicker."

Lydia did not want Tessa's instructions to spur her on. She almost ran up the drive, and was waiting at the gate long before she saw a car in the distance, and knew it was Harold Taylor.

He drew up and, without getting out, opened the door and held out his hand to help her in beside him. His car was only a small one, a grey two-seater, but to Lydia at that moment it seemed a haven of refuge.

"Where shall we go?" he asked.

"Anywhere," Lydia answered impetuously, "Just drive; anything to get away from this house."

He did as he was commanded, and for some moments she did not speak to him, only let herself sink back against the cushions.

His face in profile to her looked stern, but she knew he

85

would never worry her, never ask questions as another man might in the same circumstances.

'He doesn't know what I have come here to tell him,' she thought, 'but he will wait until I am ready, showing a consideration that very few men would offer.'

With a sigh Lydia pulled off her hat and put it on the floor at her feet.

"Where are you taking me?" she asked.

"I thought we might go out towards the Pyramids," he answered. "You aren't in a hurry to get back, are you?"

"I never want to go back," Lydia said vehemently.

Major Taylor took one hand from the steering-wheel of the car, and held it out to Lydia. She put her own into it and felt as his brown fingers closed over hers a comforting sense of being protected.

They drove on for some way in silence until, in the distance, Lydia could see the Pyramids rising from the flat golden desert, standing solid and imperturbable against the blue of the morning sky.

"I expect you think I am being silly and hysterical," she said in a small voice.

"I don't believe you are capable of being either," Harold Taylor answered softly.

He drove until they reached the desert, where they turned aside from the crowds of tourists, camels and donkeys, and hawkers that cluster round the foot of the Pyramids, and went on until they were alone with only the golden sand stretching towards the far horizon.

There they could see the Pyramids standing majestic in their defiance of time and the frailty of man, and ignoring the futility of those who try to commercialize their splendor.

It was still and very lovely. A mirage shimmered in the sunshine. Lydia sat silent, conscious that the beauty of the East could always for a moment soothe away her difficulties and her troubles, however tiresome or personal they might be.

Then as she realized that Harold Taylor was waiting patiently beside her, she turned to him with an effort, and started to tell her story.

CHAPTER TEN

'What am I to do?" Lydia asked.

She had finished telling him of her anger with Gerald, and her despair at making Ann see the foolishness of her actions.

"There are only two people in the house that I care about, Ann and Tessa. They are both young, both at the beginning of their lives, and the surroundings in which they are bound to contaminate, probably ruin them.

"Perhaps it is silly to care as much as I do, but I can't help it. I can't stand by and see Ann ruin herself with a man like the Baron, or watch Tessa alternatively neglected and spoilt by that fiendish mother of hers."

Major Taylor took out his cigarette case.

"May I smoke?" he asked.

She nodded her assent. He lit his cigarette.

"I know a great deal about Baron Sébale," he said slowly; "you haven't exaggerated in the slightest degree the danger of his association with Ann. It must be stopped, but how to do it is another matter. Gerald Carlton is the proper person to speak to Sébale, but whether he will do so is quite another matter. Has he any sense of responsibility, I wonder?"

"You warned me, you know," Lydia said; "at least, I guessed a good deal from what you left unsaid. How right you were. But I wish you had said more, and that Ann and I had turned around and gone back to England."

"Has the child no guardians except her mother?" Harold asked.

"I don't know," Lydia replied. "Her mother is, of course, her natural guardian. I believe that Sir John left

87

Ann's money in the hands of trustees until she is twenty-five. One could, of course, appeal to them."

"I doubt if they would help very much," Major Taylor answered; "the Baron isn't a fortune hunter. He is an exceedingly rich man with vast estates both here and in France.

"Another difficulty is the fact that he is welcomed by Ann's stepfather, and to all intents and purposes by her mother, to their house.

"Were he to carry on a secret flirtation with the girl, as he would be bound to do if she lived in any other household, we could make a genuine scene about it; he's not accepted by any decent woman here; but in this case he is quite safe, and he knows it!"

"But suppose Gerald Carlton did turn the Baron out of the house," Lydia suggested. "Would Ann—or he—accept the position quietly?"

"Things would be much easier," Harold answered. "Public opinion could make it impossible for him to go on seeing Ann."

"Then you will have to speak to Gerald," Lydia said.

"But what could I say that would carry any weight?"

"Perhaps he will listen to you. I have done my best, and it has not had much effect," Lydia said, with a bitter smile.

"It is hardly my business," Major Taylor said, hesitatingly.

"Oh, but you will try to make him see sense? Please, Harry, please say you will."

She used his Christian name quite inadvertently, and perhaps it was that, combined with her pleadings, which made him turn towards her and say earnestly:

"You know I will do anything to help you, anything in my power. I will speak to Gerald Carlton, I promise."

"Thank you," Lydia said, and she put out her hands towards him gratefully.

He took them in his, and to her surprise bent his head and kissed them, one after the other.

For a moment she was silent, then, nervously attempting to hide her embarrassment, started to talk of Tessa.

"Tell me about her father," she asked.

"He's a cousin of mine," Harold Taylor answered. "I knew him only slightly, for he was in the Navy while I was a soldier. He was very popular in the Service—one of those charming people who make friends wherever they go.

"It was when his ship was stationed at Malta that David met Nina. She was pretty and pathetic, two things which he could never resist.

"Once they were married, she assumed new airs and graces and a way of expecting unlimited credit which would have been horrifying to anyone except the empty-headed fools with which she surrounded herself.

"When David came home on leave she made life miserable for him, and finally she asked for a divorce.

"David agreed, partly because he was so unhappy and partly because he still believed in the old code that no gentleman divorces his wife.

"It was only when things had gone too far for him to retract that he realized that under these circumstances Nina would keep Tessa.

"She made a great fuss about the child, thinking she would get more money if Tessa lived with her. She was right, as usual, and she received an allowance for the child which is quite out of proportion to David's income."

"But it's disgraceful!" Lydia interrupted; "she never does a thing for Tessa, most of her clothes are in rags, and, as you know, the child has never had any education."

"I had no idea things were so bad," Harold answered. "Until you came out here I kept out of Nina's way. But now I do know I have written to David, telling him about his daughter, and suggesting that he applies to the Courts and cuts off Nina's allowance."

"I hope he does," Lydia answered. "Tessa is getting older, and she is an intelligent child. She doesn't like her mother now, but in a few years she will begin to realize exactly how bad she is. Oh, I am so glad you have written."

Major Taylor smiled. "Are you happier?"

"Much!" Lydia replied; "it has been such a relief to tell you everything."

"You know I would do anything I could to help you," he said again.

"I couldn't think what to do," Lydia answered, "I felt so lost, and so frightened, until I remembered you."

"I wish you would always remember me."

"I will," Lydia said lightly.

Harold Taylor turned round to face her.

"I mean all the time, in every way," he said in a low voice.

In almost panic Lydia realized that he was speaking seriously and earnestly.

She tried not to look at him, but in spite of herself her eyes were drawn to his face, and she read there what his shyness was preventing him from putting into words—that he loved her.

'At all costs,' she thought desperately to herself, 'he must be prevented from proposing to me now. I can't bear to refuse him, and I don't want to accept him.'

With a quick movement she opened the door beside her.

"I must get out for a moment," she said. "I am cramped with sitting for so long."

She stood with her feet in the soft sand, feeling the soft wind from the desert fan her cheeks. Far away in the distance a small caravan of six heavily laden camels was setting forth on a journey.

Lydia felt the call which every Eastern traveller experiences, the desire to find some place unmodern, uncontaminated by the influence of the West.

There was romance, there was a thrill in the thought of finding somewhere across hundreds of miles of sand people for whom time had stood still since the mighty Pharaohs built the Pyramids, since Cleopatra sailed the Nile in her barge with its sails of purple silk.

"I want to look at the Sphinx," Lydia said.

Leaving the car, they walked past the three great Pyramids until they came to where the enigma stood, its face towards the sunrise.

There was that strange, mysterious smile on its mutilated face—a smile comparable only with that of the Mona Lisa.

Lydia stood and looked in silence. She tried to guess as millions have done before her, the true symbol of the Sphinx, to explain its strength and its mystery.

To her the Sphinx stood for love, love not only of a man for a woman, the love of passion and the love of procreation, but also the love of the Divine, that which raises a man up to his highest self, until he finds there the likeness of God and knows that he can never rest until it be attained.

She gave a deep sigh.

"We must go back," she said, "it is late," and they walked towards the car.

"When will you see Gerald?" she asked, when once again they were sitting side by side.

"I will come now, if you like," Harold answered. "I have got some work to do this evening, and I shall be busy this afternoon, so if he's in it would be really more convenient."

Lydia looked at her watch. In spite of what seemed to her the passage of hours, she saw it was not yet eleven o'clock.

"He will either be at home or at the Club," she said.

As they neared the house they saw ahead of them two riders. Their horses were walking slowly, and the man was bending towards the girl, her face upturned to his, her fair hair catching the sunshine in the curls which clustered round her neck.

"It is the Baron and Ann," Lydia said, 'they are later than usual this morning."

"We won't stop," he said calmly. "They seem fairly intent on each other. They won't recognize you."

"It will be better if they don't," Lydia said. "I would hate Ann to think I was spying on her."

Harold was right. Neither Ann nor the Baron looked up as the car passed; Lydia glanced at them; she saw that Ann was smiling, and that she looked happy.

The Baron was decidedly smart in his riding kit, and his horse was a magnificent grey of Arab blood.

His face was in profile to Lydia, but there was something about the sharp outline of his jaw, and in the dark lashes veiling his eyes, which gave him a sleek, feline look, and she understood so well why Dandy said he was stealthy.

He was, and it was the stealth of a panther stalking its prey, moving softly but remorselessly through the long grass, every muscle alert, every nerve strained, ready to spring, yet waiting with inexhaustible patience for the right moment and opportunity.

91

When they reached the house Lydia got out of the car, and leaving Harold to ring the bell and ask for Gerald went straight into the garden in search of Tessa.

She found the child some way from the house down by the river's bank, sitting on the ground cuddling a stray cat in her arms, and singing a song to herself.

She gave a cry of pleasure when she saw Lydia, and ran towards her still clutching the thin, unhappy-looking cat.

"Look what I've found in the shrubbery," she said, "I have given it milk, and I am going to keep it as a pet."

"It may belong to somebody else," Lydia suggested.

"Well, if it does," Tessa answered, "they're very cruel; the poor thing is half-starved. Just look at its bones."

There was no doubt that the cat had not been fed for some considerable time.

It was not a pretty cat, with a wild look in its green eyes, but Tessa had obviously brought it confidence and comfort, for it lay purring in her arms, making no effort to escape.

"I have christened it Barnado," Tessa announced. " 'Cos it's a waif and stray."

"A very appropriate name," Lydia said, laughing.

She felt sorry for Tessa, knowing the longing of every child for a pet. In all probability the cat would slip away at the first opportunity, despite the bribery of milk and food.

"Has Uncle Harold come back with you?" Tessa asked. "Can I go to him?"

Lydia shook her head.

"Not at the moment, darling," she answered. "He's with Uncle Gerald, and they want to talk business."

Tessa sighed.

"I do love Uncle Harold, don't you?" she asked.

Lydia laughed.

"I think he is very nice," she answered.

"But don't you love him?" Tessa insisted.

"When you are grown up," Lydia answered, "you don't say you love somebody; you say they are nice instead."

"Mummy doesn't!" Tessa retorted, "she is always madly in love with someone. She tells every one about it. My last Nanny used to listen for hours and hours, and then

92

the young man that Mummy was in love with ran away with someone else, and she sacked Nanny because she said she hated servants knowing too much."

Lydia sighed. These sort of confidences from Tessa were always difficult to answer. The child made them so spontaneously and with a *naïveté* which made it difficult for her to oppose them.

"Suppose you go indoors, Tessa, and get a book," she said. "I will read to you."

"All right," Tessa answered, "but I will tell you something else, Aunt Lydia. Mummy thinks Uncle Gerald is in love with you. I heard her say so this morning, and she was awfully angry with him about it."

Without waiting for Lydia's reply, Tessa, still clutching Barnado, ran towards the house. Lydia stood staring after her as though turned to stone.

She was afraid, and this time she knew she could not turn to Harold for protection.

CHAPTER ELEVEN

It was very quiet in the garden after the noise and chatter in the dining-room.

Lydia felt as though she dived into cool green water as she stepped from the lighted verandah into the dusk of the night.

High above the voices she had left behind she could hear Nina Higley's laugh, and the shrill voice of Tessa who, in spite of her protests, had been allowed to stay up for dinner.

The guests were all men, of the type abounding in Cairo —hard racing, hard drinking, and hard living.

They were the sort that Nina considered amusing, and she laid herself out to be more than usually flirtatious and ingratiating, until Lydia had suggested that she should take Tessa up to bed.

Knowing that it would annoy Lydia, Nina had calmly answered that Tessa could stay as long as she liked, and had added:

"If you want to go, please do, Mrs. Bryant. I am sure you have a lot of duties to see to."

Lydia flushed at this impertinent dismissal, but rose with what dignity she could command, and went from the room.

Nina Higley's face had been flushed with wine and excitement; the men had all had a lot to drink, and the subjects of their conversation and for their laughter were not for the ears of a child of Tessa's age.

But having been plied with sweets, and being allowed by her mother to drink a glass of white wine, Tessa was naughty and more precocious than usual. She was overexcited.

Lydia knew that on the following morning she would be tired, and both her nerves and vitality would be affected.

An evening like this was definitely injurious to a highly strung child. And yet she could do nothing. Nina delighted in making Tessa disobey her.

She did not always succeed, because Tessa adored her teacher, and the only person who paid any attention to her in the house; but, at the same time, it was not to be expected that a child of eight should voluntarily deny herself any spoiling which came her way.

Her mother, in her present mood, would allow her any license, and Tessa was quick to take advantage of it.

Gerald, sitting at the top of the table, had not glanced once in Lydia's direction.

He had not returned home until just before dinner, and Lydia had no idea as to what was the result of his interview with the Baron, or what had passed between them.

She had gone into Ann's room while she was dressing, and had asked her if she would give up her dinner engagement tonight, but Ann had refused.

"As far as I know," she said, "we are not dining alone. There was some talk of a party."

"Won't you ring up and ask?" Lydia had ventured, but Ann shook her head.

"Anyway, we are not dining at his house," she said, "and I can't come to much harm in public, can I? Or perhaps you think I can!"

Lydia had realized that to continue this argument would be to bring about another outburst of defiance, and rather than be antagonistic to the girl before she knew what Gerald had achieved, she thought it wiser to give in with good grace.

"Very well, darling," she said. "But you do know I am worrying for your sake, and not my own, don't you?"

Ann looked at her anxious face and suddenly smiled.

"I ought to loathe you," she said affectionately, "but I don't. I think you are just fussy and needlessly anxious. Don't worry about me, I can look after myself."

"I wish I really believed that," Lydia answered.

"Anyway," Ann went on, "I couldn't stand Nina this evening. I bet she has found out about me by this time, or wormed it out of Gerald. She will have several catty remarks to make in her usual sweet manner. If I stay here I shall lose my temper and hit her! You wouldn't like that, would you?"

"I think it would be very undignified," Lydia said.

But she smiled at the thought of the spectacle; Ann laughed outright.

"If she doesn't leave soon," Ann said, "I shall tell her exactly what I think of her—not that it will do any good. I expect lots of people have done so in the past."

"I am terribly sorry for Tessa," Lydia said.

"I can't think why your beloved Harold Taylor doesn't do something about her," Ann said, pinning a rose into her fair hair.

Lydia flushed.

"He's not my—" she started, but Ann interrupted her. "Oh, yes, he is, or at least he would like to be! It is all very well for you to talk about me," she went on. "I can't stop Ali from being in love with me any more than you can prevent us all knowing that Harold Taylor is in love with you!"

"If he is, he's not said so," Lydia said firmly.

"I bet that's your fault, and not his," Ann said shrewdly. "But I don't suppose you will be able to keep him off for ever. He will come to the point sooner or later. Do you want to marry him?"

"Certainly not!" Lydia answered. "And anyway, as I said before, he hasn't asked me."

"Well, I'm in the same boat, so wish me luck and don't be cross," Ann said, and after a light kiss on Lydia's cheek she ran down the stairs.

'She is incorrigible,' Lydia thought, and knew that she could not be angry with her for long.

She had such a gay and happy character; this love affair had made her obstinate, but surely it was a minor fault?

Lydia felt that the Baron had captivated not Ann's heart, but her imagination.

She was eager for romance and experience. He was forbidden fruit, temptation in its most attractive guise, and he played to all that was theatrical in Ann's nature.

Gerald's behavior at dinner did not reassure her as an

ally against the Baron, and she decided that if things did not improve in a day or so, she would write to Evelyn.

She would not only ask for her advice, but suggest also that some pressure should be brought to bear on Ann, even if it meant that they must return home.

'It is ridiculous that a girl of eighteen should be without proper guardians,' Lydia had thought to herself in the dining-room as she watched Gerald pour himself out another glass of brandy.

Without knowing it, her face bore an expression of disgust, and he looked up suddenly and saw her watching him.

For a moment they held each other's eyes across the table, then he looked away and made some low remark to Nina, which made her scream with laughter.

Alone in the garden Lydia tried not to think of Nina. She was annoyed and exasperated by her almost beyond endurance; her insolence was hard to bear.

It was an insult to have to remain in the same room with her when she was behaving as she had this evening.

'What would Evelyn have thought of all this?' she wondered.

She could have had no idea as to what society she was sending her and Ann.

Lydia knew how the evening would end; Tessa would fall asleep at the table, her small face flushed, her eyes, until they closed, black with tiredness and excitement.

Her mother, the worse for drink, would get more vulgar every moment, reverting to the manners of her chorus-girl days.

Finally the child forgotten or left to the native servants, the party would drive off to one of the low cabarets of Cairo.

They would pack into Gerald's car, Nina sitting on some man's knee, her arms round his neck, her voice and laughter high above the roar of the engine would be heard long after the car had left the drive and turned along the road.

'Thank goodness I needn't see her again tonight!' Lydia thought, as she walked towards the river bank.

Peace was beginning to descend on her in the cool dimness of the garden.

The night and the vast heavens above filled with stars brought new hope and strength. 'Keep faith,' they seemed to say, and Lydia knew she must not fail.

"How dare I complain?" Lydia said to herself. "How much fuller my life is today than it was this time a year ago."

How unhappy she had been, how lonely! She had no one then to worry about except herself, but her days had been empty, and her uselessness had been as much to blame for her misery as her environment.

She sat down on a low bench, wrapping a chiffon scarf which was part of her evening dress closer round her shoulders.

She found her thoughts recurring again and again to Gerald. She saw that life for him out here must be, as hers had once been, full of emptiness. He had no work, no real interests, and a man must work in some way or other if he would find contentment.

"Love can never fill a man's life to such completion that nothing else matters," she told herself, "and it is especially impossible for an Englishman."

Lydia felt that Gerald needed her pity more than her condemnation, and she felt herself giving out a warm sympathy and understanding towards him.

So vivid and so real was this impulse that she felt no surprise when she looked up and saw that he was approaching her, already but a few yards off from where she sat.

"I thought I should find you here," he said gently.

Lydia forgot their differences of the morning. Smiling up at him she moved a little to one side so that he might sit beside her.

"Where are your guests?" she asked.

"They have gone to a cabaret," he answered.

"And Tessa?"

"She has gone to bed."

"I will go in to her," Lydia said, half rising.

"There is no need," Gerald answered, putting a hand on her arm. "Dandy heard us leaving the dining-room, and came downstairs to fetch her."

Lydia was conscious of his hand on her arm, but she made no movement to release herself. His fingers gave her a vague comfort, a sense of protection which she told herself was ridiculous.

"What happened this morning?" Lydia asked, unable to bear her curiosity a moment longer.

"I spoke to the Baron," Gerald said, taking away his hand. "He first of all pretended that I was making a fuss about nothing, and then eventually, when I put things pretty strongly, he agreed that he would not see Ann again."

"She is dining with him tonight," Lydia answered.

"He told me that," Gerald replied, "but said it was a party, and that it would cause comment if Ann did not come."

"I don't trust him," Lydia said uneasily.

"Neither do I," said Gerald, "but what could I do? He agreed that Ann was too young to have herself talked about with a married man. He regretted that he was not in a position to ask her to marry him, and promised me that they would not meet again, after tonight."

"It all sounds too plausible."

"Aren't you being a little pessimistic?" Gerald suggested.

"Perhaps, but I can't believe that he is willing to give up Ann so easily. She is very attractive, you know, and very much in love with him."

"How could she be," Gerald said, "the man's a bounder of the worst type."

"I thought he was a friend of yours," Lydia said quietly.

Gerald turned round on his seat to face her.

"Look here, Lydia," he said, "I want to talk to you. I am sorry for what happened this morning. I honestly had no intention of not seeing Ann, and you were quite right to be angry, but don't you see how impossible my position is where Ann is concerned?"

"Don't let's discuss it," Lydia said.

She realized as well as he did the difficulty. There was such an obvious retaliation for Ann to make at Gerald's interference.

"Wouldn't it be better," Lydia suggested, after a moment's pause, "if you make some excuse to send Ann back to England? Among her own friends again she will soon forget this man."

"Send you both away!" Gerald said.

Lydia nodded.

"It would be much the best thing to do," she said. "After all, there's nothing really important to keep Ann here. She sees very little of her mother, you know."

"Where do you live in England?" Gerald asked suddenly.

"Nowhere at the moment," Lydia answered, surprised at his question. "As I told you before, my husband is dead, and the home which we had together has been taken back by his family. The family don't wish to concern themselves with me, or I with them. If I am out of a job I shall go straight to Evelyn Marshall."

"In Worcestershire?" Gerald said softly.

On an impulse, without considering her words, Lydia said:

"I have seen your home. I went there with Evelyn."

There was a sudden tense silence. Lydia felt the man beside her had stiffened, and she saw that his hand, which had been resting on the seat between them, was gripped until the muscles shone white.

"What did it look like?" Gerald asked after a moment. His voice was low.

"Very beautiful," Lydia answered, "but empty, and . . . lonely."

"You know that I can't go back," Gerald said.

He spoke sharply and loudly so that his voice rang out into the stillness.

"I understand," Lydia answered.

"Then why tell me?" he asked fiercely. "Why make it worse by talking about it? Can't you see that I have tried to forget?"

His voice accused her more than the words he spoke.

"I'm sorry," she whispered.

"Oh, my God!" he said.

The wild anger seemed to leave him; dropping forward on his knees beside Lydia he encircled her with his arms, and hid his face against her. For a moment she quivered in his hold, then she was very still.

"I love you!" he said brokenly. "I loved you from the first moment that you came walking into that room, so different, so utterly different to everybody here. You were everything that I have dreamed of for so long.

101

"You looked like home and England come to me. I have wanted them so, and I want you. Oh, Lydia, my darling, don't be cruel to me!"

Beyond words, Lydia pressed his head close against her breast, touching his hair with gentle fingers, trying to comfort him.

"How can I send you away?" Gerald went on. "How can I lose you? I am tied, but I love you—I love you."

"Hush!" Lydia said, trembling. "Don't tell me—you mustn't."

He obeyed her. For a long moment they remained in silence, their arms around each other; then he got slowly to his feet.

Lydia could see that his face was white and drawn, and there was an expression of suffering in his eyes. She rose too.

They stood looking at each other and, as their eyes met, some fierce passion held them spellbound. Lydia was trembling, yet she could not take her eyes from his.

He drew her nearer to him, and with a sound which knew no language but was a cry of love, of triumph, and of suffering, seized her in his arms.

He held her pressed against his heart, and his mouth sought hers. She felt his kisses—fierce, possessive, demanding, they swept her into the sky and the world was forgotten.

She felt a sudden rapture streak through her like lightning; she felt that her whole being was surrendered, utterly captive to the fiery touch of the man who held her.

It was a moment of madness, of wonder, of ecstasy, only when they drew apart again, the radiance faded from Lydia's face. She was so pale that Gerald put out his arms to steady her, but with a sudden cry she put her hands up to her eyes.

"My darling, have I hurt you?" he asked.

He would have caught her to him, but she stopped him with a weak sound of refusal.

He waited, but she could not answer him, could not control the sobs which rose on her throat, choking and blinding her.

With a little gesture of her hands she thrust him on

one side, and turned towards the house. He could have stopped her, but he knew she would not wish it.

Stumbling because of her tears, Lydia reached, after what seemed to her a long time, the sanctuary of her bedroom.

She closed the door and locked it before she flung herself down on the bed, crying as if her heart would break.

CHAPTER TWELVE

For long after Lydia had left him Gerald stood beside the river.

He had no regrets for the lack of control which had made him confess his love to her; he knew that he could not have stopped himself had he tried.

His pent-up feeling and emotions had burst from him with a violence like that of tropical rains blotting out reason, logic, even thought.

He knew, too, that his desire for Lydia, for her coolness, her sanity, and her reserve, was not only physical, but something which had become a part of himself.

From the moment that he had first seen her he had known that he wanted her, and while she had stirred and reawakened the memory of all that was past, his present and his future seemed bound to her.

He had not really been aware until he had seen Lydia how cruelly he was still suffering, and must continue to suffer, for having taken Margaret away from her husband.

Looking back over the years, he knew without pretence or self-pity how very little, how absurdly little, he had obtained in return for the price he had been obliged to pay.

His love, which had seemed so powerful and overwhelming at the age of twenty-two had been, it was easy to see now, mere physical desire sharpened and made more intense by the glamour that surrounded Margaret, her beauty and her position.

The big grey castle, and the heirlooms which had hung for generations on the walls, the well-trained servants, and her taciturn, difficult husband, were a set background for her pink-and-white and gold beauty.

She was the princess in the fairy tale who must be

rescued, and Gerald, at twenty-two, was caught into a spell of her casting and of his own imaginings.

The months of subterfuge were hard to bear. Gerald had been brought up to be straightforward, to loathe lies, to dislike anything dishonest or dishonorable.

When he went to Taverel Castle, ate Sir John's food and watched his host at the end of the table, he felt unclean.

He would like to have gone to him after that first night of his and Margaret's together and told him the truth. She had scoffed at the suggestion.

At first Gerald could not believe that this love of theirs was only to be a clandestine affair in which they must pretend, lie, and scheme if their happiness were to continue.

Gradually even Margaret, robbed in an armor of her own selfishness, was aware that Gerald's ardency was flagging. He no longer seemed as eager as she for the nights when her husband was away.

Finally, she faced the fact to herself that she must either go away with Gerald or lose him.

Because she was tired of her present life, afraid of growing old and terrified of loneliness, she told Gerald that they must elope.

Gerald still loved her, but his emotion at the news was not the same rapture with which he would have greeted such a suggestion two months earlier.

He had grown older and a little disillusioned in the interval. But—never for one moment did it occur to him to draw back from that to which he had committed himself.

It took Gerald exactly six months to know and to admit to himself that their elopement was a failure. Sir John made it perfectly clear to them both, through his solicitors, that he had no intention of parading his name through the divorce courts.

Margaret was dissatisfied, querulous, and inclined to blame Gerald for leading her into such a position. There was nothing to be done and Gerald was the first to realize it.

Fortunately they had plenty of money, for Gerald had been left a small fortune by his grandfather, and his parents had made no attempt to discontinue the very adequate allowance they had always made him.

After drifting around Europe the two of them gave up hope that Sir John would change his mind; they tried India, Burma and Java in search of amusement.

Margaret did not make things any easier by flirting with other men. She laid herself out to be alluring to them almost as feverishly as though, Gerald thought later, she had some presentiment or intuition of what was to come.

Gerald had always been sensitive, and he had been used all his life to that atmosphere and environment of respectability and authority which was the foundation of his home.

He had never known before how much the respect of one's fellow men mattered.

Sitting now by the side of the Nile he knew why he was afraid to go home, even now when Margaret and he were married.

It was not the county people he minded, he could meet the insults and recriminations of his own class. But the village—he could not face the village, because he had let down the people who had known him since he was a child.

Gerald could not explain to himself exactly why Lydia had brought back to his memory with so much vividness the life and the people of Little Goodleigh.

It was something in Lydia herself; in her eyes which seemed to have suffered, yet to have come through suffering to an understanding; and in her voice which reminded him so vividly of his mother's with its low, gentle tones.

He had hated Margaret's voice from the day he had heard it giggling from the verandah of a bungalow in India.

He had come home unexpectedly to find her in the arms of a man he had until then respected. It was not the first time that he had been aware that Margaret was seeking other love than his.

The man who was kissing Margaret was the Colonel of a well-known regiment. He was a bachelor, and it had therefore been easy for him to offer Gerald and Margaret his friendship, despite the wives of the regiment who refused to call.

Gerald had liked him. He was a much older man, who had the knack of being popular with all ages and classes of men.

Gerald had entered the house quietly and he stood there a moment staring at his wife and at the man to whom he had given his friendship. Without a word, he went to his own room.

They had no idea that they had been seen, and as he turned to leave them he heard Margaret's voice say:

"Oh, my dear, kiss me again!"

Sitting on his bed Gerald asked himself what he should do, and knew that he could do nothing. He felt suddenly very young—Margaret was thirty-four, the Colonel was over forty, he was only twenty-three.

How could he interfere? How could he ask two people immeasurably his senior to apologize to him? Had he any right to ask it? He was not Margaret's husband, only her lover.

Thinking of the woman he still loved, of the sensuousness in her voice, and of the abandonment of her white arms curved around the Colonel's neck, he felt physically sick.

He had a wild desire to walk out from the bungalow, to take the first boat home to England, to leave this woman to any man who cared to take her. But he knew that for honor's sake he could not.

He was tied to her by far more insoluble bonds than those that could be forged by church or law. Margaret was his now, his to protect, to take care of—for ever.

The words of the marriage service came to his mind to mock him—'For better, for worse, till death us do part!'

When finally Gerald and Margaret were to hear those words it was under very different circumstances to any that they had anticipated in their wildest imaginings.

Margaret knew then that she was a hopeless cripple for the rest of her life. Famous specialists from every country had examined her and pronounced her incurable.

She would live, they told Gerald, and there was every likelihood that she would live for many years, but she would never be well; they could not offer the faintest hope.

They were in Cairo; it was there that Margaret had had her accident, and when she could be moved from the hospital they settled into a small house with a large garden, and tried to reconstruct some kind or semblance of a home.

Margaret received a letter to say that her husband was dead. When she read it she laughed for the first time for many months, but it was a bitter, miserable, humorless sound.

"It is too late now," she said to Gerald, and he knew that she spoke the truth.

The first woman with whom he was unfaithful to Margaret was a Russian. She was dark, thin, and rather vicious. He hated her because she excited him, and he was grateful to her because for a short while his mind let him rest.

The Russian woman was the first of many. He offered them presents and passion but never his confidence or his love. But they loved him. There was something about him they could not resist.

Perhaps his indifference helped, perhaps the feminine instinct in each one of them knew that deep in this man there was somethinig they could not reach, could not understand.

They worried him with their jealousy, they irritated him with scenes which ended eventually in anger and separation.

Always he offered them only the Gerald Carlton whom Cairo knew, but never the boy who had gone down the drive of his home so many years before to a clandestine meeting from which he had never returned.

CHAPTER THIRTEEN

Baron Sébale went home from the Club after his interview with Gerald in a bad temper.

He cursed the servant who opened the door to him, he called for a whisky-and-soda and was furious because the man took a second longer to bring it to him than he considered necessary.

Outwardly to Gerald he had kept a suave demeanor, protesting that he did not understand the meaning of what he insinuated.

Ann, he assured her stepfather, could come to no harm in his company. But beneath an easy manner, and a smiling friendliness, he was furiously angry.

He told himself that he despised Gerald—a man who was fool enough to marry a woman many years his senior, who lived a rotten immoral life among second-rate people.

Why should he, a millionaire, a man of considerable standing both in France and in Cairo, mind what this Englishman, who was disapproved of by his own people, said or thought?

Yet he did mind.

There was something in the Gerald who spoke to him in the Club who commanded his attention in spite of himself.

This was not the man he had seen carried home drunk from parties, or whose private life was the joke of the gossiping community. This was a man—grave, serious, and surprisingly dignified.

Ali felt like a small boy summoned before his schoolmaster. He had the same feelings of impotent rage, of being defiant but silent. There was nothing he could say —Gerald, he recognized, was right both morally and conventionally.

Gerald's few words had inflamed the hatred of all Englishmen which, quite unknown to those with whom he associated, was a vital part of the Baron's character.

His father had chosen for his instruction, during his holidays from a French school, English tutors. One of them many years ago had lit this fire of hatred which had ever since smoldered fiercely.

The tutor, an undergraduate in need of funds, had been an excellent athlete but stupid. He did not care for the dark handsome boy whom he was to coach during the holidays.

Ali was soon aware that on some subjects he knew much more than his tutor. He took the greatest delight in sharpening his wits at the Englishman's expense.

It amused him to expose his tutor's ignorance of women—Ali's experience was already considerable, and with shrewd intuition, he guessed that his tutor was innocent, as well as uninformed. He tried to shock and surprise him; he succeeded in disgusting him.

The young Englishman itched again and again to give the boy a thrashing; instead, he conscientiously tried to educate him not only in mathematics, but in conduct which he had been brought up to regard as the mark of a gentleman.

Going to bed one night rather later than usual he heard muffled cries coming from Ali's bedroom.

For a moment he hesitated, wondering whether it would not be better to go straight to his own room rather than to interfere.

It might be a trick, but if it were not he debated whether he would be acting within his jurisdiction. A succeeding cry was, however, piteous; he tried the door to find it locked.

"Open the door," he commanded.

Ali shouted in defiance:

"Go to bed and mind your own business."

But the subdued anger of several weeks was aroused and the placid young man had lost his temper.

Putting his shoulder against the flimsy woodwork, the tutor broke it in.

He found—as he had expected to find—one of the servants, a pretty country girl who had but lately come to the house, weeping bitterly in a disheveled state while Ali in pajamas and dressing-gown faced him furiously.

"Get out of here," the tutor said to the girl in French. She made an effort to obey, but Ali seized her by the arm, refusing to let her go.

"Get out of here yourself," he shouted. "You have no right to interfere with me in my bedroom."

The girl made a violent effort to free herself, crying hysterically, her long hair falling over her bare shoulders.

"Let her go, you damn' swine," the Englishman cried and he hit Ali with all his force.

As he fell backwards to sprawl on the floor, Ali recognized the superior strength of the man who had hit him, even while he loathed him with a murderous hatred.

Work was continued the next day as though nothing had happened, but Ali from that moment had a fanatical dislike of the English and everything to do with them.

He spent much of his life at his father's home in France, but in his visits to Cairo he was well aware of the environment from which he had been bred.

His father, old and senile, cared only for women. His mother refused to leave the house or mix with Europeans. She believed that women should be kept in purdah.

She did not seem to mind or resent other women who came to the house. She was happy in her own room with her maidservants, eating the many native sweetmeats which made her grow fat as the years of inaction went by.

She had long ceased to interest her husband; it was his son whom he adored and he spoiled the boy in every possible way.

At seventeen Ali had an allowance which would have seemed a fortune to an ordinary European of the same age; race horses of his own, cars to drive, and any woman that particularly took his fancy—he bought them all.

His father would chuckle and laugh when some girl brought to the house for his own amusement was captured by young virile Ali.

The house had once formed part of a palace, and though it had been added to and enlarged it still bore the characteristics of its former state; towers, carvings and mosaics, hundreds of tiny rooms, and narrow windows which excluded the sunshine.

Like the East, in its very existence it seemed to breed intrigue. Of those who lived there, the outside world knew nothing; the sensuous enjoyments to be found within its walls were guessed at by prying cold-blooded westerners, for the Baron and his son had no confidants.

Ali learned of love in his home—not the love of a man for a woman, but the love of a prince for a slave.

There were in the rambling palace many women—all his for the taking. Women experienced in the art of passion, women of every age, many in their dark-skinned immaturity breath-takingly lovely, yet he found himself turning away from them to the fair passionless girls who visited Cairo in the cold weather.

It was perhaps inevitable that his hatred for English should resolve itself into a desire for their women. He wanted to subdue them, to conquer them, and to know that in their surrender he was master.

Ali's marriage had at the time made a stir. He had met Yvonne de Brelac in Paris and had been attracted to her immediately, not because she was French, but because in some way she looked so English.

She came from Normandy and she had a fair complexion, brown hair with glints of gold in its depths and the blue eyes which are not rare on those seafaring shores. She came of good family.

They were married in Quimper Cathedral with all the pomp of a Catholic service. Ali wanted Yvonne to go to Cairo with him for their honeymoon, and as it was the right time of the year she happily agreed.

When she arrived in Cairo she was afraid of her husband; by the time she had spent two or three days in his home she was a girl horror-stricken almost to insanity.

She had no idea of what she was to find; Ali's talk of his home had been drawn almost entirely from his imagination.

The small, close rooms, the dark women moving amongst them, the old Baroness herself, gross and toothless, were enough to frighten any girl.

What was worse, her husband's lovemaking appalled her. She became for the first time conscious of her body and she shrank from this new aspect of herself, afraid of pain and afraid of pleasure.

114

Everything seemed to her unclean, obscene and terrifying, she had only one wish—to return home.

She was merely a child and more innocent than Ali could have believed possible. He had charmed her into marrying him but he had no idea how to charm her into loving him.

When they told him she had run away he laughed, and when he received a letter from her father saying that she would never return he shrugged his shoulders. He soon forgot about her in the pursuit of other women.

Ali knew that the attainment of his desires gave him no lasting satisfaction, but while his desire was there he was tenacious and crafty, planning a coup with a cunning which he must have inherited from some Oriental ancestor.

From the moment that he had first seen Ann he had wanted her. He had thought that she would be easy to capture, but in the pursuit of her he found himself growing increasingly excited by her coolness and self-confidence.

All that was savage and untamed in him rose when he thought of her. The fair golden hair which he wanted to grasp with fierce cruel fingers; the unclouded blue eyes which met his so confidently; the red mouth which as yet had no understanding of passion or of kisses.

Never, Ali told himself, had he ever been so thrilled before; never had he been so determined that a woman should be his. But he was wary; he knew that English women were not easy—they were so often sensuous with their minds but unmoved by their bodies.

They had a way of evading capture just when one thought that one had them completely at one's mercy.

Ali would think about Ann for hours on end. He would concentrate on her; he knew that he must be clever—that he must not frighten her away. Like a man scattering crumbs before a bird-trap, he approached her gently with stealth and cunning.

It was perhaps this fierceness underlying his calm, poised exterior which attracted Ann. Without a true knowledge of what it meant she sensed that she wore a mask in her presence.

Ali waited, alert for the moment when victory would come.

But now, when he knew that she was genuinely falling in love with him, when the prize lay within his grasp, he had been told to leave her alone.

Ali, lying on a couch, lit cigarette after cigarette, his half-shut eyes seeing in the haze of cigarette-smoke Ann's upturned face, her blue eyes liquid with the dawning of love.

A few more meetings and then ... Ali rose to his feet, with a gesture of impatience he kicked a gold-and-velvet footstool from him, then he suddenly stood very still, an idea had come to him.

Four people were dining with him tonight—respectable well-chosen people who would make the evening a jolly but by no means rowdy one.

Ann would have liked them, but he would easily have been able to hold the conversation, to make himself shine, the only person present so far as she was concerned. It was to have been one more step in the right direction, another point in his favor.

But time was short. This might be the last night that Ann would be able to see him. He believed that she would come tonight; she had sworn on all that she held holy that nothing or nobody would prevent their dining together tonight.

He had been very humble in his pleading. But he had been afraid this morning that something might upset their plans. He had sensed danger when Ann had told him that there had been trouble about their drive to the Pyramids.

After Gerald's interference she might not come, but if she did it would be for the last time.

He must act swiftly. Picking up the telephone he spoke to the two couples who were to have been his guests, and made his apologies that the dinner had been cancelled.

Leading from his sitting-room was a dining room where he breakfasted, and where those more favored of the ladies of the household were, on occasion, entertained.

This room was to be decorated in pale-pink roses. They were to be massed in great bowls, garlanded and wired

116

into shape until the walls of the room were partially concealed. It was to be a bower—a frame for Ann.

His orders were repeated by the servant, and only when he was alone again did Ali permit himself to dream; he would have his own way.

When he thought of Gerald he thought of him as a whole army of Englishmen ranging right back to his tutor who had knocked him down many years before. They were standing in his path, all forbidding him to take Ann, all threatening him by their quiet even tones and level gaze.

He would defy them! Ann should lie in his arms that night. He would seize her, take her and make her his. He might bring fear to those candid unclouded eyes, he might make that confident red mouth cry out, but he would be the victor!

Ali stood looking at himself in the glass; he saw there not the dark hair brushed away from the broad forehead, the handsome features, the sharp-cut chin and sensuous mouth, but only the dark eyes of an Oriental. It was the East in his blood that wanted Ann.

The West let their women go about unprotected, unguarded, and a temptation to men's desires, and the West was shocked and surprised if a woman thus brazen was violated. The East should once again defy the West.

"Ann will be mine," he told himself.

He knew that stronger than his desire, stronger even than the passion mounting within him, was his unquenchable thirst for revenge.

CHAPTER FOURTEEN

Lydia's love for Gerald was a fire burning through her, consuming every thought, and leaving her emotions as steel tried by the flames, steadfast, strong and without a flaw.

It would have been impossible for her to question her love, she knew it was there, and she was of it.

Yet, while she could not think of herself, she could think of him, and by looking at him with new eyes, with a vision vouchsafed because of the glory that was in her, she saw what she must do, and what was the right action for her to take for his sake.

She had to resist the temptation to give herself to Gerald, to forget the world, his wife, his stepdaughter and all that stood between them. Never for a moment did she seriously consider it.

Love such as she felt could come only from God Himself, imbued with His Spirit, and could work only towards all that was perfect and ideal.

When she had run away from Gerald, she had wept because of the love which swept over her with the violence of physical pain. She could not for the moment stand up to such force, it overwhelmed her.

Only when her nerves were stilled did the wonder of it come to her, healing, soothing.

Gerald was hers, Lydia knew that, even as she knew that she belonged to him, not only now but for all time and forever. Whether they lived together, or whether they never saw each other from this moment, there was no question of their one-ness.

They were no longer two people, they were part of each other.

A miracle had happened to them, but there were still earthly ties which could not be dissolved; chains which once forged must remain until removed by Divine intervention.

It seemed to Lydia then as though a voice was counseling her, calming her mind, preparing her for a message.

She had no idea what it might be, but she knew that when it came to her it would, because of the source from which it came, help Gerald to solve his difficulties.

She flung wide the shutters which covered her bedroom window and the great silver moon high in the heavens bathed her in its radiance. The whole world had a new quality.

She knelt against the rail of her balcony feeling the cool stone beneath her knees. The moonlight touched her head in blessing.

As she knelt, sending forth her whole being towards the Power which had given her so much more than she dared to hope for, there came to her the message for which she had been waiting.

'Gerald must go home!' The words were spoken in her heart, they echoed in her mind.

He was being a coward. He had shouldered so many responsibilities that he could not shirk those few more that must be added to him. Margaret was now his wife, and their home was waiting for them at Little Goodleigh.

Gerald was traveling in the wrong direction. She knew that he would not refuse, could not refuse her. This message had been sent to her to show him the way and he would not fail.

When Lydia rose from her knees she felt as though a great load had been lifted from her shoulders. Everything was clear. The whole future seemed as unclouded as the sky to which she raised her face.

It seemed hard to step back into her bedroom—it was as though she went back into her daily life from some communion with God.

She turned to go, thinking that it must be late and that she must try and sleep, when a knock came to her door. Without waiting for an answer the door opened, and Ann came in.

She was wearing a long white brocade coat with diamond buttons and she held it tightly around her, almost strained across her chest as though close-fitting it could give her a sense of protection.

She stared at Lydia for a moment in silence. As though with a great effort she appeared to bring her thoughts to what she was about to say. In a voice dead of any emotion, low, yet curiously distinct, she said:

"I want to leave here tomorrow."

Lydia was taken by surprise.

"Tomorrow?" she echoed. "But, my dear, where do you want to go—home?"

Ann shook her head.

"Not home," she said, "but anywhere else, anywhere you like as long as it's away from here."

"But, Ann!" Lydia started to expostulate, "it's so sudden, I can't think like this . . ."

Something made her stop. Some instinct told her that she should not ask questions but agree. Ann had the appearance of someone who had experienced a shock.

She did not look at Lydia as she spoke and her eyes she kept lowered so that it was impossible to read the expression in them. 'What has happened?' Lydia asked herself, and felt a fear clutch at her like an icy hand.

"Of course we'll go, darling," she said, "if you want to. We must just make some plans as to where we shall go and how."

"Constance Martyn is going up to Khartoum," Ann said, still in that strange voice which seemed to come from far away and be entirely detached from her.

"Very well," Lydia agreed, "we'll go there. I will be up early and see about tickets."

"Thank you," Ann said politely as though to a stranger.

She turned towards the door, Lydia put out a hand to stop her.

"Ann, darling," she said, "what is the matter? Do tell me."

Ann pulled her arm away from her restraining hand as though it were a serpent.

"Don't touch me," she said violently, and without another word went from the room.

All her fears and apprehensions returned in an overwhelming force. What had happened tonight to make

121

Ann look like that? Lydia searched for her watch, it was just twelve o'clock. She had not been away long, for she had not left the house until nine o'clock.

No lover's quarrel could make her look so strange, so unlike herself—Ann was a different girl from the one who had defied her chaperone earlier in the day, who had taunted Lydia with Gerald's omission to keep their engagement.

When she thought of Ann the questions that she would not dare voice came to stand round her bedside so that she could not avoid them.

She saw Ann, she saw the Baron with his stealthy smile. Ann's voice haunted her. She hid her face in her pillow and whispered:

"Not that, dear God, not that!"

CHAPTER FIFTEEN

Lydia and Ann spent the following night in the train.

They embarked at Shelal in a steamer, spending the next two days and nights on the broad Nile, passing Abusimbel with its great rock temples, and the flooded half-submerged villages, victims of the new Assuam dam.

At Wadi Halfa they boarded another train to cross the 250 miles of desert on the railway made for Kitchener and his advancing troops in '98.

They arrived at Khartoum as the sun was sinking into the desert. After the dreary barren wastes through which they had been travelling it was strange to see the well-built modern town, with its prosperous white houses and avenues of green trees.

Lydia stepped out of the carriage a little bewildered, dusty and tired after the long journey.

"Hello, Constance," said a cheery voice, "I am pleased to see you."

Constance Martyn who had spent the journey in the company of Ann and Lydia, gave a shrill cry of delight.

"Tony!" she exclaimed. "Darling, isn't this exciting?"

She flung her arms around the neck of a tall sunburnt young man in khaki.

"This is my brother," she said a moment later to Ann and Lydia. "Tony, meet two angels. I should have had a perfectly damnable journey if it hadn't been for them."

Tony Martyn smiled and stammered his thanks. He was shy with the delightful deprecating shyness of a man who is more at home among men than a crowd of women.

"My man will see to your luggage," he told the travellers. "I have got a car to take you to the hotel."

It was a big open Chevrolet and Constance jumped into

123

the front seat beside him, leaving Ann and Lydia to sit behind.

"Tell us all the excitement," Constance chattered as they drove away from the station. "You got my wire telling you to expect Ann and Mrs. Bryant, didn't you?"

"I did and I have told everyone. You will all get a splendid welcome, I can promise you. It has been awfully dull out here the last month or two, too hot and some *haboobs* to make things worse."

"What on earth's a *haboob?*" Constance asked. "Do talk intelligently, Tony, I can't bear it when you go all native."

Tony Martyn laughed. 'Sandstorm, then, if that pleases you better."

Constance turned round in her seat.

"Tony is just like all the people who live abroad for long," she said. "He speaks pidgin English if we don't stop him. When his regiment was in India he came home talking in such a 'Poona-Poona' way that we had to give him hell to cure him of it, didn't we, darling?"

"Not half as bad as you were after you had been to New York," her brother retorted. 'You had an American accent that one could cut with a knife for at least six months afterwards."

"You are a liar!" Constance said rudely. "Don't take any notice of him, Lydia, he never speaks the truth."

Lydia was amused at the badinage between brother and sister. During their four days' journey she had grown to like Constance. She was young and enthusiastic about everything, like Ann had been before . . . But here she drew up her thoughts with a jerk! She would not voice her fears, not even to herself.

Ann had been strangely silent ever since they left Cairo. She had sat still for hours at a time, staring ahead of her but with unseeing eyes.

She was reserved, aloof, with an uncanny calmness that was so unlike her and utterly alien to her character. She had not confided either in Lydia or Constance, and had resisted all efforts on their part to draw her back to her own natural effervescent self.

"What on earth's wrong with you, Ann?" Constance had asked. "She looks as though she had seen a ghost."

"I didn't know anything was the matter," Lydia answered lightly, "but I expect it's indigestion, or a touch of the sun."

But when they reached Khartoum she found herself watching Ann.

"What is wrong with the girl?" she wondered.

Ann looked so pretty, her fair hair slightly ruffled after the hat she had been wearing had been thrown carelessly aside, the pale blue of her dress reflecting the blue of her eyes.

"Will you all come and dance after dinner at the Club?" Tony asked. "There's a gala evening there tonight. You know, the usual sort of thing, a band from the regiment, a floor on the lawn and fair-lights, but it's quite fun and I'll get a couple of fellows to make us even numbers."

"Oh, we'd love it," Constance said before anyone else could speak, "wouldn't we, Ann?"

Even Ann seemed unable to resist the prospect of a party.

"I would like to come," she said gently without looking at Tony.

When they had gone to the ball and Lydia waited for her lonely dinner she relaxed in the long chair beside the open windows. She took up a book but she could not read.

For the first time since she left Cairo she allowed herself to think of Gerald and of her farewell to him.

She had risen early in the morning and been at Cooks as soon as the doors opened to take tickets and ask for reservations on the train and on the boat.

It had not taken long, and when she returned the household were only beginning to get up. Seeing a servant on the verandah, Lydia called to him.

"Go to Mr. Carlton," she said, "and say that as soon as he is dressed, Mrs. Bryant would like to speak to him. I will wait for him in the garden down by the river."

She walked across the lawn and down the wide grass path which led to the Nile. Flowers were opening in the sunshine, bees were busy humming from blossom to blossom, there was still a freshness in the air which would in a few hours be dispelled by the heat of the sun.

Lydia felt happy, not yet could she face the thought

that the evening would mean separation from Gerald. It was very quiet, she closed her eyes from the glitter of the sunlight on the water.

She opened them at the sound of a footfall. Gerald was coming towards her. He was in riding clothes and she thought how attractive he looked.

He did not smile in greeting, the expression on his face was one of strain, yet it seemed to lighten at the sight of her. There were lines round his eyes which told her he had not slept.

She put out both her hands to him with a little gesture of surrender. He took them in his, kissing first her fingers, then pressing his lips against the palms, lingeringly, passionately.

"My precious darling," he said, and his voice was hardly louder than the murmur of the bees.

"I love you," Lydia said gently.

There was such a radiance in her face as she spoke that Gerald felt he could not look at her and bowed his head again to her hands.

"Oh, my sweet," he murmured.

Lydia sensed that his words were a cry for help. She knew that he was struggling against the barrier that divided them.

That he was longing for her as she for him, but with the difference that he did not as yet see that their love could come to them only through sacrifice and in honor.

Holding tightly on to his hand, not looking at him as she spoke but across the wide waters of the Nile, Lydia said:

"Gerald, darling, you must go home."

He was shaken by her words, too surprised at first to protest. She went on talking, without argument, but gently, persuasively, until gradually he began to see that she was right.

Only once did he say in a voice so low that she could hardly hear the words:

"But can I face it without you?"

"It is not really without me," she said tenderly, as if she were speaking to a child. "I am with you always, my darling. From now on my thoughts, my prayers, all of me that matters or is of any importance belongs to you. It

126

is only bodily that we may not be . . . united . . . not yet."

"I need you so," he said.

"And I need you," she answered, "but we know that it cannot be, not perhaps until we have made ourselves worthy of this love which has been given us."

"You are right!" He spoke abruptly.

She could feel the whole man stiffen as a soldier to attention.

"I am not worthy of you, not yet, but I will be. And I swear now, before God, that my whole life from now on is dedicated to you."

His whole expression seemed to change, he was a man transfigured, the lines of dissipation were dispelled by a firmness, and a determination.

The old ideals came to life, the knighthood within Gerald that had been lying dormant was resurrected. He knew that what he undertook was to be a hard fight which would require all his courage and his faith, but he accepted the challenge willingly.

Lydia had pointed the way and although he was afraid, although he shrank with every sensitive nerve of his being from going home, he knew it was the first step in a new life and that he must go.

Then Lydia told him that she and Ann were leaving for Khartoum.

"Perhaps it is better," she said softly.

But she was unable to prevent the tears gathering in her eyes as she spoke. This was good-bye.

"So soon," Gerald said involuntarily.

Then he stood up and drawing Lydia to her feet, put his arms around her. He held her encircled, close to his heart. But for the moment he did not kiss her.

He looked down at her upturned face, memorizing the serene beauty of the calm, unlined forehead, the dark grave eyes, and sensitive mouth.

"Good-bye, my true love," he said, "the only woman in the world. I love you now and for ever."

Slowly he bent his head to press his lips to hers. For a moment they were completely united. Lydia felt as if her whole soul fused with Gerald's.

She was no longer an individual, no longer apart from him. Her heart and mind became his. The world was forgotten, they were alone in unbelievable ecstasy, caught in a flame of wonder and joy.

There was no time, for they tasted eternity. They were conscious only of the glory of which they were a part.

He kissed her forehead, her eyes, her cheeks, the little pulse beating wildly in her neck and then again her mouth.

Then he looked down into her eyes.

"You are in my mind, my heart, my soul," he said, "and I am yours for all eternity."

Then he released her.

"God bless you, my perfect love," he said, and his voice broke.

They walked in silence together back towards the house.

CHAPTER SIXTEEN

"No-one can talk of anything else except you," Tony told Ann, forgetting his shyness for the moment, "and all the men are furious with me."

"Why?" Ann asked innocently, looking up at him as they danced in the crowded ballroom with its high windows opened to the starry night.

"Because you let me bring you here tonight," Tony said, smiling down at her.

"I had seven other invitations," Ann said, "but of course I came with you; I had promised, hadn't I, the very first night I arrived?"

"I was afraid you might chuck me," Tony confessed.

Ann laughed.

"Oh, no," she said. "I am a girl of my word, at least, generally."

"I think you are wonderful!" Tony whispered.

His face was pink at his own daring, but he guided her steps skillfully to avoid a couple who were self-consciously doing intricate steps in the middle of the floor.

Then as the music stopped, he drew her out of the ballroom on to the wide balcony.

Ann was enjoying herself. It was lucky that they had arrived in Khartoum in time for the Palace Ball.

Already their engagements were following one upon the other until they never had a moment to themselves.

Even breakfast parties were arranged for them, and although Ann protested that it could not be done, she had found that such sociability was quite easy, because the two girls nearly always rode at seven o'clock in the morning.

They managed to get a little rest between two and four, then there was quiet, and the British colony went to bed.

It was an unforgivable sin to telephone or call during those two hours, and Lydia was insistent that her charges should not chatter, but really make up for some of the beauty sleep they lost by dancing until the early hours of every morning.

Tony had managed to lure Ann from her utter despondency.

She was regaining her laughter, Lydia noticed with relief, and only occasionally would she find the girl with that brooding, heavy look in her eyes, and have her questions answered in monosyllables by a voice from which all life seemed to have fled.

Ann smiling, with shining eyes, in the Palace ballroom was a very different person from the Ann who had sat silent and aloof during the journey from Cairo.

"Let's go into the garden," Tony said to her.

It was possible at the Palace to dance in two places. There was a floor in the garden, and one in the ballroom. They had sampled both, and also been to the long buffets erected on the cool, open verandahs which, built of white marble, ran along every floor of the building.

The Palace was white, and the scarlet uniform of the servants, the great vases of colored flowers, and the diamonds and decorations made the whole scene appear to have come straight out of a fairy story.

Obedient to Tony's suggestion, Ann led the way down the broad steps to the garden.

Here there was the sweet fragrance of flowers growing in rich profusion, and the soft, romantic music of a waltz being played by a uniformed regimental band.

Ann slipped her arm through her partner's and they turned aside from the crowd to wander down the grass paths and under the shade to the banyan trees.

"I am enjoying myself," Ann said.

"Are you really?" said Tony in a strange voice.

He put his free hand over hers as it lay on his arm, and she felt the strength of his brown fingers.

She gave him a quick, startled glance, and started to talk at random, chattering about this and that. Tony hardly seemed to hear her. He was nerving himself for the most tremendous step he had ever taken in his life.

In spite of his attraction for women, about which his sister teased him unmercifully, Tony was a very humble person.

He loved his work, enjoyed the Army with an enthusiasm which made him popular not only with his senior officers, but with the men who served under him.

He was also a fine athlete—rugger player, and champion of his battalion at golf, he played tennis and squash as a matter of course. He had played for Harrow at Lords.

It was a joke among the senior men that Tony was so entirely oblivious of the women who ran after him. But now at last he had fallen in love.

He thought Ann the most beautiful person he had ever seen in his life, and since she had come to Khartoum he had not slept for thinking of her, while she had been in his thoughts every hour of the day.

He drew farther and farther into the shade of the trees. She was still talking, but suddenly she seemed to realize where they were going.

"Let's go back to the ballroom," she said hastily. "I shall be cutting dances if we go too far."

"Ann!" Tony said desperately, "I want to talk to you."

"But must you talk now?" Ann answered, looking back the way they had come.

"I must," Tony said. "Ann, I love you, will you marry me?"

The words tumbled out of his mouth, falling over themselves in their very sincerity. Ann's carelessness fled, she grew pale. Hardly aware of what she did she turned towards him.

"Oh, Tony!" she said; then their arms were round each other.

They clung together more like two children than a man and a woman.

"Is this really true?" Tony stammered at last, his cheek against Ann's, for he had not dared to kiss her.

With a sudden bitter cry she tore herself from him. Pushed him away with outstretched hands.

"It isn't true," she said. "I can't marry you."

Without another word she fled from him, her white tulle dress flowing out behind her so that she seemed in her swiftness hardly to touch the ground, but to be on wings.

Tony stood staring after her, too surprised to attempt to stop her, too startled to do anything but watch, his heart thumping, his hands clenched.

He stood tense and still for a long time after she was out of sight; then with a sob he could not control, turned and put his hot forehead against the cool trunk of the great tree.

"Oh, Ann!" he said despairingly.

She did not love him, he told himself. He had been a fool to think that she might. Why should she care for him when with her beauty and her attractions every man in the place was mad about her?

She had everything in life, looks, youth, money, and freedom. Only sometimes during the past days had he wondered if she were completely happy.

Sometimes she would seem sad, and there had been a wistful droop of the red mouth that he had longed so desperately to kiss. He wished that he had had the courage to ask her what was wrong; he would like to share it with her, to help her, and protect her.

She was so tiny, it seemed to him, so slender and small, and every instinct in Tony cried out to be allowed to guard this exquisite, fragile creature from anything that might harm her.

He pulled himself together. He must accept this disappointment. Perhaps she would relent, perhaps change her mind. After all, she had come to his arms quite willingly.

She had put her arms around his neck and let him hold her. That was something, at any rate. She must like him a little even to give him that.

Tony blew his nose violently and with a casualness that he did not feel walked back towards the Palace.

* * * *

Ann ran until she reached the crowd of dancers entering and leaving the Palace.

Then she slowed her pace, but slipped quickly through

132

them until she reached the huge, cool hall hung with wide swords and shields of bygone days.

Here she hesitated for a moment, remembering that she and Lydia had come to the Palace in Tony's car.

Her indecision was noticed by one of the native servants waiting in the doorway. He came towards her, and impulsively she made up her mind.

" I want a taxi," she said.

"Very good, Miss." He raised his hand to his forehead in salaam.

Ann hurried to a nearby room where the ladies' cloaks had been left. She found hers, a wrap of satin and ermine, and, slipping her arms into the wide sleeves, she drew it closely around her.

The taxi was not long in coming, but Ann felt as if she could hardly wait for it, but must rush out into the darkness.

She wanted to be alone, to be able to shed the tears which were welling in her eyes in spite of every effort at self-control. She had not cried for years, but now a flood of hysteria was sweeping over her.

Would the taxi never come and take her away from prying eyes?

At last the servant returned, and she slipped past him and into the waiting vehicle.

"To the hotel," she said abruptly, and they started off.

Now that she was alone she found the relief that she had imagined would be hers in tears and in the abandonment of her control was denied her.

She could not cry, only clench her fingers together and stare ahead with wide, aching eyes.

It was only a few moments' drive to the hotel; she paid the taxi with some loose silver, and walked up the steps towards the verandah.

The terrace was deserted, and the hotel in darkness and silence. There was a dim light coming through the glass panels in the front door; there was no sign that anyone was awake. With her hand on the door to pull it open she hesitated, and turned round again, looking towards the river, where it flowed serene and calm the other side of the road.

She felt restless and agitated. Now that the desire

for tears had passed, she felt as though every nerve within her was strung to breaking point. Her head throbbed, and she had a wild wish to scream.

Moving slowly, she retraced her steps. She crossed the road, and stood under a lebbakh tree. The night wind was whispering in the leaves, lifting them with a weird rustling sound, otherwise all was quiet.

"I love Tony!" Ann told herself.

She wondered what he was feeling, what he was doing. He would be searching for her, she thought, wandering among the dancers, hoping every moment to catch a glimpse of her.

His good-natured, sunburnt face would be anxious, there would be a comical cockle between his eyes which he imagined was a frown when he was concentrating deeply, but which Constance assured him only made him look humorous.

"I love him," Ann repeated.

He was very dear to her—she knew that now. She loved his tenderness, his kindness, and the way he thought of her, never of himself. He was so big and strong, yet sometimes clumsy like a boy who has not yet confidence in his own strength.

"I love him!" Ann whispered again, and the leaves above her seemed to whisper the words.

Yet how could she tell him so? How dare she return the love that he offered her?

With a shudder which shook her whole body Ann covered her face with her hands. Vivid, brutal in their intensity, memories came to her of what had happened in Cairo the night before she and Lydia had left. That day stood out for her as vividly as an etching.

She saw herself gradually being involved in the net which had been so subtly spread for her. She saw herself deliberately entering the snare which had been skillfully laid.

What a fool she had been. Why had she not listened? Why, indeed, had she not understood what Lydia had tried to tell her?

Now it was too late, too late to undo what had been done. Too late to go back and become the happy, carefree girl she had been before she met the Baron.

Why, why had she allowed herself to be taken in by him?

Something had paralyzed her mind. It was as though she stood staring into a bottomless black pit. She could not raise her eyes from it, must go on staring and staring. And she might sink, might be lost in that dark, evil . . .

Her life had stood still, her consciousness had ceased to function . . .

Afterwards, she had dressed herself, she ate, she slept as though she were an automaton. Part of her worked mechanically. But she knew that waiting for her was something terrible, cruel and bestial—and she was afraid.

It was Tony who drew her back, as it were, from a long twilight into the land of the living, but he gave her back also the capacity to suffer.

She had felt nothing until now, she had been sunk in lassitude and despondency which encircled her so completely that she believed the world outside would never be able to touch her again.

With Tony at her side and the knowledge that she loved him came the throbbing of her awakening emotions. With them was the horror from which subconsciously she had shrank—fear, terror, and the torture reliving the past.

"I can't bear it," Ann told herself.

It seemed to her that she was being torn in bits. The agony was too great. The fear that had consumed her in the Baron's house swept over her now.

It was a fear so real, so vivid, that to Ann it stood beside her, grasping at her with greedy, senuous fingers, compelling her to surrender, dragging her into its clutches.

With a choking cry she moved forward from the shelter of a tree. At the edge of the embankment she stood looking down into the dark water swirling and eddying below.

"One step more," she told herself. "One step more."

She was mesmerized by the rhythmic movement of the river, by the glint of light and shade, by the soft sluch of moving water.

"I shall escape," she whispered beneath her breath. "I shall forget."

Something seemed to tighten in her head, to press against her burning eyes . . . With a cry which was only the whimper of a frightened child, she threw herself forwards . . .

She hit the water with tremendous violence, and felt it close over her head.

"I am going to drown," she told herself.

But the instinct of self-preservation was too strong. She struggled.

The water blinded her, and the force of her fall had for the moment taken away her breath. She floundered, spluttering and bewildered, until she realized that her feet were firmly embedded in the mud.

She was soaked to the skin, her evening cloak heavy and sodden over her shoulders. She stood, shaking and trembling, and found that the water reached barely above her knees.

Hardly knowing what she was doing she dragged herself nearer to the side of the embankment, which rose sheer some ten or twelve feet above her head.

Leaning against it she tried with trembling fingers to press back the wet hair from her face. Suddenly she was sick.

The feeling of nausea and dizziness passed. She knew that she must somehow clamber up to the level of the road. Dimly she remembered that there were steps.

Holding on to the wall with her hands, she forced her way through the cold water. It took her a long time.

She rested, leaning exhausted against the embankment. The water was bitterly cold, her clothes were so heavy that, after a time, she dragged off the evening coat and threw it into the river, watching it carried away from her on the current, away in the darkness, growing smaller until it was lost from sight.

She thought it would be easier to move without it, but the wind was cold on her neck and arms. She was soon shivering so violently that she could not even control the chattering of her teeth.

At last, when she felt she could go no farther, must cease from trying, she saw ahead of her the narrow stone steps. She climbed them on her knees. When she reached the top she lay exhausted.

After a long time, with a tremendous effort she dragged herself to her feet.

"I must get to my room," she told herself. "I must get to my room!"

She forced herself down the road towards the hotel, fighting against utter weariness which might at any moment overcome her. Time stood still.

The short distance to the hotel seemed endless. Finally, the lighted door of the hotel was before her.

She reached out her hand to push it open; it required a last stupendous effort from her.

Only as she saw the familiar hotel lounge and the startled face of the night porter did she lighten the hold on her consciousness. Then swayed and, without a sound, pitched forward to the floor.

The darkness which was within herself encompassed her, and she knew no more.

CHAPTER SEVENTEEN

"Is Ann going to die?" Tessa asked as Lydia tucked her into bed and kissed her good night.

"I hope not, darling," Lydia replied, but she felt the tears come to her eyes.

"Is she very ill?" Tessa asked.

"I am afraid so."

"I am praying that she will get well," Tessa said earnestly, "and Uncle Harold is too, I asked him."

"We must all pray," Lydia said.

"I always pray for anything I want," Tessa said confidently. "Do you remember when God made Uncle Harold take me out riding after I had asked Him?"

"Yes, I remember," Lydia said, her mind going back to those days in Cairo when she first knew Tessa.

"Uncle Gerald prays too," Tessa said suddenly. "I didn't think he did somehow. I thought he was like Mummy. Mummy doesn't believe in God."

"How do you know he prays?" Lydia asked. She could not stop herself asking the question.

"Well, one day," Tessa said, cuddling down in her pillows, "I was playing in the bushes with Barnardo—you know, the bushes down by the river. We were playing Red Indians, and while we were hiding, waiting for someone to scalp, Uncle Gerald came along.

"He sat down on the seat and I was just going to jump out on him when he sighed and looked terribly sorrowful. I can't explain exactly, but he looked sad, really sad. If he had been a woman I should have thought he was going to cry, but then men don't cry, do they, Aunt Lydia?"

"Not very often," Lydia answered.

"So I thought perhaps he wouldn't want to be disturbed. So I held Barnardo very tight and we just kept still. Uncle Gerald sat for a long time, at least it seemed a long time to me because I was sitting so very still. Then suddenly he said quite loud: 'Oh, God, make it come true!' That must have been a prayer, mustn't it, Aunt Lydia?"

"I think it must have been," Lydia said.

She bent to kiss Tessa, holding her tightly so that the child should not see the tears which could not be checked any longer and which welled into her eyes and onto her cheeks.

Tessa hugged her.

"Shall I tell you a big secret," she said.

"Yes, do!" Lydia answered, striving to make her voice sound natural.

"Well, it is very wicked of me," Tessa said, "because I am awfully sorry about Ann, but I can't help being a teeny-weeny bit glad too, because then, you see, I can stay up here with you and Uncle Harold, and I do love it so."

Lydia hugged her again. It was a fortnight now since Tessa had arrived in Khartoum with Harold.

Ann had been desperately ill, getting steadily worse for besides the pneumonia, she had what the doctors described as a mild attack of brain fever and was continually delirious, screaming and crying out in a frightening, heart-rending way. She recognized no one.

Lydia had been increasingly glad that Harold was with her. She would have felt so utterly alone and the responsibility would have been too great without someone by her side.

She had telephoned Cairo and got on to Dandy who had told her that Gerald was out, but she had fetched Harold, who had just been riding with Tessa, to the telephone.

Nina Higley had walked out on her child soon after Lydia and Ann had left Cairo and Harold had wired Tessa's father.

He had replied saying he would get leave but in the

140

meantime would Harold make provision in some way or another for Tessa.

Harold knew it was impossible for Gerald to travel to Khartoum but he had solved the problem himself by bringing Tessa with him.

Ann had been removed from the hotel to a private nursing home where Lydia spent most of the day waiting patiently in case she should be needed.

Dr. Watson had become a firm friend. He kept her calm and hopeful about Ann, and when she knew him better, he showed her some of his work that he was attempting to do in Khartoum. Disease was being stamped out by his unceasing vigilance.

The natives trusted him, and his progress with the women was gradually breaking down the horror of dirt and superstition traditionally attendant at childbirth.

Tony was perhaps the most fortunate of those who waited so anxiously for Ann's recovery. He had his work to do and he had not got to sit, as Lydia had, day after day with idle hands, too nervous to leave the home for any length of time.

But Tony's usually cheerful face wore a perpetual look of anxiety, and his companions missed his cheery laugh which had been such an inevitable part of his conversation.

As soon as he was free in the afternoon he would come down to the home. Lydia grew to know the sound of his car and the deep note of his horn as he rounded the corner and drew up at the gate.

A moment later he would come striding across the lawn to her.

If Harold was there she would persuade them to go down to the Club and have a game of squash—anything she thought to stop Tony from brooding.

She herself had grown thin with anxiety and there were deep lines under her eyes which told of nights spent without sleep.

It would have been impossible not to think of Gerald during those hours of solitude. A letter which Harold delivered had brought her tremendous comfort, she had not replied, but it was with her always, both night and day.

It had not been a long letter, only a few lines, but it told her everything that she wanted to know.

"My precious darling, this is to tell you that I am thinking of you always, and because you wish it, I am making arrangements to leave here as soon as possible. When I go, you will be with me too, always in my heart and in my thoughts. God keep you, my Lydia, I love you.

Gerald."

'In England,' Lydia thought, 'they would be getting ready the Manor to welcome its master.'

How she wished that she could be with him! Could anything be more thrilling than to return home after many years of exile?

She wondered how Margaret would stand the journey, but she could not imagine her feelings or emotions at being back.

Margaret was so apathetic about everything that Lydia could only think that this change would mean little to her, would affect her only as regards her comfort and not in any deeper way.

Evelyn would meet them. There would be at least one pair of hands outstretched in welcome, one smiling familiar face to greet them on arrival.

Harold had kept in touch with Gerald over the past days and he told Lydia that Margaret was not aware of the seriousness of her daughter's illness.

"Dandy thinks it might bring on one of her heart attacks," he said. "She gets them very badly, you know. When she was first injured she was in almost continual pain and they were obliged to give her too many drugs to keep her from such terrible suffering. It affected her heart and that is why the nurses and doctors insist that she should not be worried in any circumstances, however serious."

"I understand," Lydia said, and again she was sorry for Margaret.

Kissing Tessa good-night she pulled the curtains over the now shuttered windows and turned towards the door.

"Good-night, darling," she said. "Sleep well."

"Good-night, dearest Aunt Lydia," Tessa answered in a sleepy voice.

Already her eyelids were dropping, she was half asleep.

Lydia went downstairs to seek Harold, and found him as she expected, sitting out on the verandah, a whiskey-and-soda in front of him, a newspaper in his hands. This was the time of day Lydia most enjoyed, when the sun sank in a blaze of glory and the darkness fell swiftly.

"Have a drink?" Harold said to Lydia, rising as she approached him to pull a comfortable arm-chair to the small table by which he was seated.

"I think I will," Lydia answered. "I am tired tonight, it has been so hot all day."

Harold ordered her one and asked: "Tessa go to bed quite happily?"

"She's asleep by now," Lydia answered. "Isn't it extraordinary how she has changed up here with us? She is getting so good, it is really no trouble to look after her. I am very fond of her."

"I am fond of her, too," Harold said.

"She adores you," Lydia said with a smile. "You really ought to adopt her. It would be good for both of you."

She had spoken lightly without choosing her words, but Harold took them quite seriously.

"I wish I could," he said, "in fact, I would if you will help me."

She knew what his tone rather than his words implied. She tried to think of an answer, but before she could do so, Harold leaned forward in his chair.

"You know what I mean, Lydia, don't you?"

She met his eyes frankly.

"I am sorry, Harold dear," she said, and put out a hand to touch his arm gently. "I do understand, but I am afraid I can't help you in that way."

She felt Harold stiffen, knew that he braced his muscles as though to guard against a blow. He stared straight ahead of him.

"I hadn't much hope, really," he said in a low voice.

"Please try to understand," Lydia said pleadingly. "I like you so much, you have been such a marvelous friend to me, but—I don't love you."

"If we were to wait?" Harold asked hesitatingly.

Lydia shook her head.

"I love someone else," she said. "There isn't a chance of our getting married, but he is the only person who could ever matter to me in that way."

She paused, then put out her hand towards him again.

"I am very lonely, Harold," she said, "and I do need your friendship."

He gripped her hand until it hurt. She saw that he was incapable of speech, that it was impossible for him to put into words what he felt, what he was suffering at that particular moment by her refusal.

The arrival of her drink created a diversion which she welcomed gratefully, but when the servant had left them again it was difficult to break the silence.

It was an effort for him to smile at her but he managed it. He took up his glass too, and raised it.

"To your future, Lydia," he said quietly, "and to your happiness."

CHAPTER EIGHTEEN

Ann was better. More than three weeks passed before she was sufficiently conscious to know Lydia and to give her a weak but welcoming smile as she came into the room.

"We have got her on the right road at last!" Dr. Watson told Lydia when she came to the hospital one morning. "She has had a good night and she will soon be her old self again."

Lydia could hardly believe the good news. It seemed to her years rather than weeks since the night of the Palace Ball.

Weeks of finding no encouragement in Dr. Watson's grave reports, weeks of presenting a calm confidence she did not feel to Tony and Tessa.

She trusted Dr. Watson implicitly; he told the truth to her frankly, neither mincing his words nor trying to raise her hopes. She liked him for his honesty, and she grew to know his verdict by the expression of his face before he spoke.

When Dr. Watson told Lydia the good news, after her first moment of wild rejoicing, she asked him anxiously:

"How much does she remember? Has she spoken about . . .?" She stopped, hesitating for words.

"There is every chance," he answered, "that what occurred before she was ill will be completely forgotten. In cases like this I have often known the entire events of a previous year vanish from the patient's memory.

"Sometimes it returns, but only vaguely, induced mostly by conversation or the people with whom they were associated.

"In the majority of cases they either awake with everything clear in their minds or the whole episode which has brought about such an upheaval in their natures is forgotten as though it never occurred."

"Let us pray that will happen to Ann," Lydia said.

"She will remember you," Dr. Watson went on, "very likely Tony and anyone who is associated in her mind with pleasant things, but the rest will have gone."

There was no doubt that Ann did remember Lydia when she went into the room to see her. Her face lit up with some of her old radiance.

She made a weak gesture towards her with her hands, and spoke in a voice so low that Lydia had to bend to catch the words.

"I am glad to see you—have I been ill for long?"

"Just a little while," Lydia answered, not wishing to tell her how long it really was. "But you will soon be up again now."

Looking at Ann she was afraid that she was being optimistic. The girl had always been thin but now she had lost so much weight that her white skin seemed almost transparent, her cheek bones and the line of her jaw startlingly prominent.

The fair hair brushed back from her forehead was lifeless. Only her blue eyes, seemingly enormous in her small face, retained their former beauty, and some echo of their old vitality was creeping back into them.

Lydia was only allowed to talk to Ann for a few moments, but before she left she asked one question which she felt would give her some idea as to how much Ann remembered one way or another.

"Would you like to see Tony?" she said.

For a moment Ann looked puzzled.

"Tony?" she whispered and then she added: "Yes, of course, dear Tony, I would like to see him very much."

Lydia knew from her calm expression that Ann did not connect Tony with anything that meant unhappiness.

It must have been on the impulse of the moment, and Lydia thought that the comparison of her love for Tony with what had been an infatuation for the Baron might have been too much for her to bear. She would have felt unclean.

146

She would have felt that she could not marry Tony with a dread and terrible secret on her conscience.

All that Lydia imagined could only be surmised, only the one thing was certain that Ann had been shocked and horrified at what had occurred that night in Cairo.

'Now,' Lydia thought, 'we will never know what it was.'

It was better, much better that it should all be forgotten, lost in the oblivion of Ann's delirium. And not only for her sake but for Tony's also.

When Ann was well again there would be every probability of her learning to love Tony. Indeed, Lydia felt she would find him, in his devotion and adoration, irresistible.

Lydia had watched Tony these past weeks, and she felt that he was the very person who could make Ann happy and prove a sensible husband for her.

Ann needed somebody with an instinct for what was true and honest as well as somebody to love her deeply. Tony would keep her from being headstrong and impetuous.

They would never do anything very great or very noble in their lives, but developing along conventional lines, they would make the world a pleasanter place because they had lived in it.

Lydia and Dr. Watson had been very careful to keep from him any hint that her delirium could have been caused by anything save the shock of falling accidentally into the river.

"She must have wanted to be alone after you proposed," Lydia said. "Any girl would want to think, to consider—and as far as I know this was Ann's first. She got too near to the edge of the embankment, stumbled and fell."

It sounded a lame explanation, but Tony accepted it without comment, and Lydia believed without reservation.

A party was arranged when Ann was better. Tessa, Tony, and Harold were invited to it and, of course, Lydia.

Ann, still looking very frail, was propped up in bed with a mountain of pillows behind her. She looked pretty and very young in her pink chiffon dressing-jacket and a narrow pink ribbon tied around her fair hair.

Tony never took his eyes off her, and every now and then Ann smiled at him in her old provocative manner.

'She is better,' Lydia thought to herself.

Harold was not a very gay member of the tea party but Lydia liked to have him there.

'He is his best in adversity,' she thought. 'A rock of security in time of trouble.'

Tessa, however, made up for any lack of conversational powers on the part of the others. She chattered away unceasingly, telling Ann all that had occurred in her small life since she had come to Khartoum.

She had been lent a pony; she had been for a sail on the Nile; she had been allowed to try the bagpipes by the Pipe Sergeant of the Black Watch and had succeeded in making a wailing noise which had pleased her enormously.

"It was exactly like Barnardo makes when he's hungry, and do you know, it made me quite homesick for him. You do think he's well, don't you, Uncle Harold?"

"I expect he's grown so fat that you won't recognize him," Harold answered.

"Ann needs fattening up like poor Barnardo," Lydia said. "We shall have to see to stuffing you, darling, as soon as you are up."

"You will do nothing of the sort," Ann retorted. "I have got a fashionable figure at last—all my dresses will have to be taken in for me, that will be a joy!"

"Hurry up and get well," Tony said impetuously.

She looked at him from under her eyelashes, an old trick which made her particularly attractive.

"I am hurrying," she answered. "I feel I would like to dance again."

"I am very glad to hear that!" said a voice from the door.

They all turned around to see who spoke. Lydia, after an audible gasp, gave a startled exclamation and sprang to her feet.

"Evelyn!" she cried. "It isn't true."

But it was, standing there in the doorway, smiling, assured and confident, was Evelyn Marshall.

CHAPTER NINETEEN

"I have never been more surprised," Lydia said a little later. "You are the last person I expected to see, Evelyn, darling."

"I thought it would be fun if I came without telling you," Evelyn replied. "It has only taken me four days to get here by air."

"Were you very worried about me?" Ann asked, putting her hand into Evelyn's as she sat beside her bed.

"Very," Evelyn confessed. "You are a tiresome child to frighten us all like this."

"I can't think how I got so ill," Ann said, puckering her forehead at an effort at concentration. "I think it must have been a bug."

Lydia's eyes met Evelyn's and a look of understanding passed between them.

"If it was a bug, it has been well exterminated, so don't bother your head about it," Evelyn said. "We must leave you now. Nurse will say you have had quite enough excitement for one day."

She bent down to kiss Ann.

"I am terribly glad you are here," Ann whispered affectionately. "Will you promise to have a long talk with me to-morrow?"

"Of course, I promise," Evelyn answered. "If you sleep well tonight!"

Leaving Ann, the rest of the party went into the garden.

"I have heard a lot about you," Evelyn said to Harold Taylor as they walked side by side towards the summer house. "Lydia's letters have been full of your kindness ever since she and Ann met you on the way out."

149

"I wish I could have done more," Harold answered, as usual, embarrassed at being paid a compliment.

He was interrupted by Tessa, who had taken an immediate liking to Evelyn. Taking her hand the child chattered away in her usual happy manner, untrammelled by the shyness which hampered older people.

"Did Aunt Lydia tell you about my cat?" she asked, after a string of questions about the aeroplane, England, and Evelyn's home.

"I don't think she did," Evelyn confessed. "So you will be able to tell me all about it yourself, won't you?"

'I have done one good thing by coming out,' Lydia thought, 'for if I had never met Harold or stayed in Cairo, he would never have realized how neglected Tessa was. She might have remained on indefinitely in her mother's charge until it was too late, utterly ruined; there would have been little chance of saving her from the same sort of life.'

Evelyn could take Tessa home with her when she returned. Her arrival had solved that problem.

"Things plan out,' Lydia thought, 'if one waits long enough.'

A sudden thought came to her. Evelyn would take Tessa and Ann home with her, but she would not go with them. There was no place for her at the moment in Evelyn's home—it was too near to Gerald.

She knew that he must fight his battle alone, that he must win through by himself, without her either to help or distract him. She must not interfere, must not on any account let his love for her or hers for him interfere with the task he had set himself.

She knew that in his homecoming he was laying for himself the foundations of a new life. Until he had built on that foundation, had begun to reconstruct from the ruins of the past, she must stay away.

She wanted so desperately to write to him. More than once she had started a letter, rising from her bed in the middle of the night to do so.

She had written him pages, pouring out her thoughts, her feelings and her love.

But when the dawn broke—the sanity of the day had made her look at what she had written, and realize that it had been a palliative for herself—she had destroyed all she had written.

Someday, somehow, she knew with the certainty of a deep-rooted faith that she and Gerald would come together. Until that happiness was permitted them there was so much for them both to do.

'I must have work,' Lydia thought, but she knew she could not consider another job as a chaperone.

A life of luxury and amusement and entertainment would never be her choice again. She did not want to dance, to wear beautiful clothes, to move from comfortable house to comfortable house.

She wanted something more difficult to do, something which required an outpouring and an outgiving of herself.

She was thinking deeply as she left her room and went slowly down the stairs.

Then she hesitated, and before going out onto the verandah, she went to the telephone box. She asked for a number and a moment later Dr. Watson's deep voice answered her.

"It is Lydia Bryant," she said. "Ann is quite all right. She enjoyed the party, but I am not telephoning you about her. I want to ask a favor for myself."

"What is it?" he questioned.

"Will you have time to see me tomorrow?" she said. "I could come out with you in the car when you go on your rounds, if you will be alone."

"I have got to go over to Omdurman at eleven o'clock," he said. "I will pick you up at the hotel."

"Thank you," Lydia answered. "I will be ready."

CHAPTER TWENTY

"Ann, I love you," Tony said.

He was kneeling by her as he spoke, his arms around her, his lips pressed against her fair hair.

He had come to the nursing home as usual at his first available moment. It was just before luncheon and Evelyn, who had been with Ann during the morning, had already gone back to the hotel.

Tony had met one of the nurses on the stairs and she had told him that he might go in for a few moments while she was getting Ann's luncheon ready.

Tony had meant to speak to her conventionally, to make her laugh and perhaps chatter with him as she had done before her illness.

But when he found himself alone with her and had looked down on her lying there frail, white and so lovely, he had lost his head and his voice.

He had merely dropped to his knees and taken her in his arms.

His kiss had been a very gentle one, but Ann had returned it and he knew then a happiness beyond all expression, beyond anything of which he had ever dreamt.

"I love you," he whispered again and again, and Ann, slipping a white arm around his neck, whispered back:

"Oh, Tony . . . I love you . . . too!"

They were so happy that they made no attempt to hide their joy from the nurse when she came back with Ann's tray.

She looked at their faces turned towards her as she entered the room and saw there a radiance which made her feel suddenly old and lonely.

"Please don't send him away," Ann pleaded, and she hadn't the heart to do so, though she knew for him to remain was against the rules.

She left them alone again. As she closed the door, she heard Tony say eagerly:

"How soon can we be married?"

"Just as soon as I am well," Ann answered.

"I have got four months more out here," he said, "and then the Regiment comes home. We will be sent to the south coast. Oh, Ann, do you think we could get married then?"

"Of course," she answered. "We will talk to Evelyn about it. She will arrange everything."

"You do love me?" Tony asked, holding her close to him. "Tell me again, Ann. I can't believe it is true."

"Of course I love you, you silly one," she answered.

"She is to eat her lunch!" nurse said, suddenly making them both jump as she put her head around the door. "If her plate isn't empty in five minutes, I shall send you away, Mr. Martyn. I don't know what Matron will say if she catches you, anyway."

"Leave Matron to me," Tony said, but he put a fork into Ann's hand. "Come on, eat it up."

In the end Tony helped her, for Ann was too excited to eat.

"You have got to do everything they tell you," Tony said, "because you have got to get well so quickly. We mustn't waste time."

"Oh, Tony, I am so happy," Ann said. "We will be married at Little Goodleigh. It is a darling little Church. Very, very old, and it is where I was christened and confirmed. Anyway, I shall have to be married there, or the Vicar would be awfully hurt—the living belongs to me, you see, it is my gift."

"How many more possessions have you got?" Tony asked suddenly. "Lydia said something about a house of yours in Worcestershire.'

"House!" Ann said indignantly. "It is a Castle and you will love it, Tony, I know you will."

"Look here," Tony said suddenly, "if you are a rich woman I'm not going to marry you. I have no idea what you have got, but I'm not a fortune-hunter, and I am not going to be kept by my wife."

"Tony, how could you say anything so horrid?" Tears of weakness welled up into Ann's eyes.

"Darling," he said hastily. "I'm a brute. I didn't mean that, I promise you."

"I can't help my beastly money, can I?" she said. "We'll give it all away to somebody who really needs it."

Tony hugged her.

"You aren't to worry," he said. "Don't you take any notice of me. I expect really I am frightened of you being too independent."

"I will never be that, I promise you," she whispered, and, with her arms clinging to him and her soft cheek against his, he believed her.

* * * *

Lydia found Evelyn alone and as if she took a plunge into deep water, she said:

"I am not coming back with you to England."

"I expected you to say that," Evelyn answered.

Lydia looked at her in surprise and she added:

"My dear, I had a long talk with Gerald before I came out here."

Lydia clasped her hands together.

"Tell me everything," she said in a low voice.

"He told me all about you," Evelyn went on. "Why you sent him home and how for your sake he was prepared to do anything; even to reconstruct the life which he thought he had given up forever."

"I was right, wasn't I?" Lydia asked anxiously. "You do think I was right, Evelyn?"

"My dear," Evelyn answered, "when we are in love our instinct about those we care for is seldom at fault. Incidentally, Gerald is not going to find things half as difficult as he expects."

"And Margaret?" Lydia asked.

She could not help adding the question, she felt she must know about Gerald's wife.

"Margaret stood the journey very well," Evelyn answered. "As soon as she had arrived Gerald sent for the London specialist who had seen her some years ago in Cairo. He was pleased with her, but he confirmed what

155

we have always known, that Margaret can't live for very long. Death will be a welcome release."

"Until then," Lydia said gently, "I shall never go back to England."

"That is wise," Evelyn answered. "But what will you do?"

"I have arranged that this morning," Lydia answered. "I went with Doctor Watson to the hospital at Omdurman. You know its story. It was started some years ago by two Englishwomen. They fought against unbelievable difficulties: prejudice, superstition, and almost fanatical hatred. But they succeeded.

"The work they do there for the native women and for their children is wonderful. I am not a qualified nurse but there is a great deal that I can do, to help both in the hospital and outside it. When you and Ann leave for England, I shall go there."

"Oh, my dearest," Evelyn said impulsively.

She was moved and surprised at Lydia's decision. She came to her and put her arms around her.

"It is a very wonderful thing you have undertaken," she said. "God bless you and help you."

"Will you tell Gerald?" Lydia asked. "Later, perhaps, I will write to him. Just for the moment I can't put into words my feelings, and they are probably much better left unsaid."

"He is working very hard to become worthy of you," Evelyn said quietly. "He told me quite frankly what his life had been. How he was sinking lower and lower, drinking and wanting only one thing—forgetfulness, until he met you.

"I had no idea of course," she added, "when I sent you and Ann out to Cairo what you would find there. It was, perhaps, stupid of me not to have made more inquiries, but Ann, as usual, was so impulsive that I hadn't time."

"I don't want you to think for a moment," Lydia said hastily, "that my love for Gerald is giving me anything but happiness. I am incredibly, wonderfully happy, Evelyn. I know that we must be separated, but that doesn't lessen the happiness of loving him or alter the knowledge that he loves me.

"One day, perhaps, we shall be allowed to be together to make a home for each other. Until then, we both have work to do. You will help him, won't you?"

"In every way in my power," Evelyn promised, "you know I will. Gerald will find that the world is only too ready to hold out a hand in friendship, when it knows that hand will be welcomed. He will gradually lose his bitterness—he has something to live for, something to aim for."

"And because he is struggling," Lydia said, "I must work too. You understand Evelyn, don't you, that I am not ungrateful for this chance you gave me, of meeting new people, of having what you call a fling for the first time in my life, but a social existence is not for me.

"I don't understand the lure of it or the excitement. Perhaps I have grown too used to suffering to find it easy to be carefree. Perhaps I want to prove to myself that I am really worthy to be a wife . . . and a mother."

The following day Evelyn went over to the hospital. She saw the wards where Lydia would work, the room in which she could sleep, the people who would be her companions.

Both women knew that from the description that Evelyn would give him, Gerald would try to visualize Lydia in her new surroundings.

It was hot in Omdurman, the sun burned down on the markets, on the houses built of dried mud, on the shores of the river where women were washing their clothes and singing as they worked.

The hospital with its wide verandahs seemed the only cool place in the native city. The women were coming in and out of the big white doors, some carrying children in their arms, others supporting an aged relation, or being taken away by friends after a successful confinement.

There was in the whole building an atmosphere of happiness and deep content, which reminded Evelyn forcibly of some of the convents she had visited.

"Lydia will be happy here," she said to herself.

It was hard, nevertheless, two weeks later to say 'good-bye'. Lydia stood on the crowded station waiting for the white sleeping-car train to leave. In it was Evelyn, Constance, Ann, Tessa, and Harold Taylor.

Harold was to escort the women as far as Port Said and then return to his work in Cairo.

Only Lydia and Tony were to be left behind in Khartoum, and in four months Tony would be home. Then he and Ann would be married.

"Good-bye Evelyn," Lydia said, kissing her friend.

"Take care of yourself," Evelyn said to her. "I will write to you and I will tell you everything that is happening. Don't feel cut off from us, you will be in our thoughts always."

Lydia smiled, she knew that Evelyn spoke for Gerald as well as for herself.

"Good-bye, my darling," Tony said to Ann. "Take care of her, Mrs. Marshall, she is very precious to me."

"And to me," Evelyn assured him.

"Good-bye Lydia," Harold said.

There was so much in his heart that he could not speak but she understood and pressed his hand in silent farewell.

"Good-bye, darling Aunt Lydia," Tessa cried. "I wish you were coming too."

She hugged Lydia, turned to get back into the compartment but stopped on the steps of the car. On an impulse she held out her beloved doll and thrust it into Lydia's arms.

"Give that to the children in your hospital," she said. "I expect they will be awfully glad to have it."

"I know they will be," Lydia answered. "Thank you, darling."

A whistle sounded and slowly the train began to leave the station.

As it did so a Railway Clerk ran up to Lydia with a telegraph form in his hand.

"For a Mrs. Marshall," he said.

"I'm afraid it is too late," Lydia replied. "She is on the train.

The Clerk looked helpless and she said:

"May I see the telegram? You could forward it to Port Said."

"Yes, of course!" the Clerk agreed and handed Lydia the form. She opened it and read:

"Margaret died this morning." "Very peaceful end. Gerald."

For a moment she could hardly take in the words. Then the full significance of them made the sun suddenly blindingly golden.

Gerald was free! Free to love her as she loved him! Free so their future could be together.

But because she wanted him to start his new life conventionally, with the approval of the County and those who had liked him as a boy, she knew they must not meet until the proper time of mourning was over.

They could write to each other. They could express what was in their hearts without fear but she would remain in Omdurman until he was ready for her.

Time would pass quickly because they were working, and then they would be together for the rest of their lives.

"Oh, my darling . . . my darling," Lydia said in her heart. "I love you . . . and there is nothing else in the world but my love . . ."

With a radiance which transformed her face, she walked slowly back along the platform.

"I love you," she whispered again and felt that the wind carried the words across the world to Gerald.